LANCASTER COUNTY SECOND CHANCES 4

RUTH PRICE

ISBN: 1515375862

ISBN-13: 978-1515375869

TABLE OF CONTENTS

ACKNOWLEDGMENTS

All Praise first to the Almighty God who has given me this wonderful opportunity to share my words and stories with the world. Next, I have to thank my family, especially my husband Harold who supports me even when I am being extremely crabby. Further, I have to thank my wonderful friends and associates with Global Grafx Press who support me in every way as a writer. Lastly, I wouldn't be able to do any of this without you, my readers. I hold you in my heart and prayers and hope that you enjoy my books.

All the best and Blessings,

Ruth.

CHAPTER ONE

Isaac Muller sat at the head of the Lapp family dinner table in splendid solitude. He was almost too big for the chair he sat in. Both of his massive elbows were propped on the table, his chin was planted on his fist, and his round blue eyes were on the kitchen door.

Just through that doorway, Cora Lapp pulled a casserole dish from the oven with a pair of cooking mitts. The bubbling concoction trailed a fragrant scent of chicken and cream and mushrooms in the air as she entered the dining room and set it carefully down on the table in front of him.

Isaac leaned over the dish, closed his eyes and inhaled with an expression of pure bliss.

Cora smiled, feeling pleased. Her big blonde fiancé had a farmer's appetite, and was clearly enjoying the table full of dainties she'd prepared for him – all of them his favorites.

It was odd that she loved to watch him enjoy her cooking -

- she'd never thought of herself as especially domestic.

But Isaac Muller had a *magical* talent for changing her mind.

Isaac had sneaked up on her. He didn't look a thing like the man she imagined she'd marry one day. He wasn't worldly, he wasn't rich, and he wasn't at all sophisticated. He wanted a traditional Amish wife, and she'd been restless as a wild bird.

Isaac hadn't even been on her radar.

But somehow, now, here she was: she'd come to God, she'd joined the church, she'd promised to obey the *Ordnung*, and was probably going to stay in the county for the rest of her life.

Because of Isaac.

Cora smiled and shook her head. *Who would've thought?*

***

They were alone in her parent's big house. It was Sunday, and after a lifetime of being dragged to worship it felt a little odd to Cora to still be home on a Sabbath. But this was a special day. As was tradition, she and Isaac were enjoying a private meal at home while their engagement was being announced to the community.

Cora bustled back and forth from the kitchen, laden with plates: Isaac's chicken and creamed mushroom sauce, smoked ham with brown sugar glaze, mushrooms in butter, a huge chef salad with boiled eggs and black olives and pine nuts, sweet potato casserole, new peas with tiny pearl onions, crisp little fried apple pies slathered in cream cheese icing, buttery pound cake, and sawdust pie.

Cora piled the plates and dishes around Isaac, taking away the empty ones, and pushing the new ones toward him. She lifted a jug of tea and filled his near-empty glass.

She had been up before dawn that morning, preparing this bountiful meal, and the look of bliss on Isaac's face made it more than worthwhile to her. She was savoring the happiness in his eyes even more than he was enjoying her food.

He looked up at her then, and smiled with his cheeks full and his lips closed, like a child.

She giggled and dabbed at his chin with a napkin. "Oh, Isaac, you're worse than Caleb!"

When she leaned close, she couldn't resist giving him a kiss. The taste of apples was still on his lips, and to Cora, it was a perfect metaphor – how sweet and simple and *good* Isaac was.

He smelled faintly of the outdoors, of fresh laundry and grass and warm skin, and suddenly she was hungry, *too*.

She slid down into his lap and twined her arms around his neck, curling her fingers in his shining blonde hair. For the first time, she kissed him without any reservation, without worrying, without anything but joy. How she loved the taste of his skin, its subtle salt-sweetness, the firmness of his neck, that strong jaw.

She let her hands wander over his muscular back, along his shoulders, down his arms. How strong and solid he was, and how safe she felt in his arms!

Isaac dropped his knife and fork and folded her in his arms. His hands twined in her hair, softly pulling their silken cords.

That strong, steady heartbeat that she loved was palpable through his shirt now.

Cora's fingers moved to his collar, fretting the topmost button, but his hands moved to clasp hers. He shook his head.

"No, Cora," he murmured. "Let's wait. We've held out this long. I don't want to do this in your parents' home. I want it to be special. At the cottage."

Cora sighed, listening to the thrumming of her own heartbeat, and rested her brow forlornly against Isaac's. But as much as she hated to admit it, he was right. She wanted that, too.

It was just so hard to behave when Isaac was *so* adorable.

She nodded, and he helped her to stand. She shook out her skirt, and tossed her head, and looked at him with such an expression of irritation that he couldn't help laughing. "Don't worry, Cora," he sputtered. "I promise!"

"You'd better," she warned him, and sat down in the chair beside him.

"See, I have a peace offering for you," he told her. He leaned over, pulled out a mysterious box from underneath his chair, and placed it on the table in front of her. It was wrapped in shiny white paper dotted with pink roses.

Cora looked at him. "Oh, Isaac… it's beautiful."

"Open it."

Cora dimpled and tore at the paper like a child. When she opened the box, and pulled out her gift, it was the most beautiful carved object she had ever seen: it was a large oval of white pine, smoothed and polished to the consistency of silk. A bouquet of delicate flowers ringed the words from First Corinthians 13:

"Love is patient, love is kind. It does not envy, it does not boast, it is not proud. It does not dishonor others, it is not self-seeking, it is not easily angered, it keeps no record of wrongs. Love does not delight in evil but rejoices with the truth. It always protects, always trusts, always hopes, always perseveres. Love never fails."

Cora put a hand to her mouth. To her own surprise, the words went through her like a spear, because they were a *perfect* picture of Isaac. He *was* patient; he *was* kind. He wasn't self-seeking; he was almost never angered. He always protected her. In all the time she had known him, he had never failed her.

She had a fleeting, ugly vision of Matt, her former boyfriend. To go from *that*, to Isaac Muller's incredible selflessness, was a miracle from God.

Tears stung her eyes. "Oh, Isaac," she whispered. "It's *so* beautiful. It's –"

Her voice failed her. Then the light blotted out as Isaac leaned over and kissed her: a sweet, tender kiss. His big hand caressed her cheek gently.

Cora was just about to respond in kind when noise and laughter from the doorway announced the fact that they were no longer alone. Cora's little cousin Rudi shrieked, "*Ach*, they're not going to make it!" The sound was followed by a sharp rebuke from a female voice, and a resounding *smack.*

Isaac pulled back from her, and Cora put her hands to her hair.

***

It was tradition, on this special day, for Cora to formally introduce Isaac to her parents. She knew they were waiting for her.

She stood up, tidied herself, straightened Isaac's shirt and refastened its top button. She took a deep breath and looked down at him.

"Ready?"

He nodded, smiled, and clasped her hand.

Cora's parents were waiting patiently in the living room. To Cora's relief, the rest of the family had taken themselves outside to the porch, though she could hear them whispering and laughing.

Her father stood up as she entered, and held out his arms wordlessly. She went into them, blinking back tears.

Her mother reached for her hand, squeezed it.

Cora's father released her after a long moment, wiping his eyes. "Are you ready to introduce us to your young man?" he asked brusquely.

Cora dimpled. "He's waiting," she told them, and took her father by the hand.

***

Isaac was standing in the middle of the dining room waiting for them, hat in hand. He looked nervous, but Amon Lapp ignored the big hand that Isaac extended and simply took him into his arms.

"Welcome to the family, son," he mumbled.

Isaac put his hands out into the air, as if he was taken aback, and patted his father-in-law awkwardly on the shoulder.

“Let’s eat,” Mrs. Lapp suggested.

CHAPTER TWO

Cora shot little glances at Isaac all through the family meal: he was quiet, almost subdued. There were two permanent red stain marks on his cheeks, and it was clear that he was overwhelmed by her loud, talkative family.

Cora suppressed a sigh. There were no less than 20 people at the table with them, and more if you counted the children's tables in the adjoining rooms. The noise of everyone talking all at once was near-deafening, and all of her relatives were curious about Isaac, and often leaned over to ask him a question or to include him in the conversation.

Poor Isaac, Cora thought sympathetically, and reached for his hand. He looked down at her in relief, but his blue eyes had a glazed, deer-in-the-headlights look. His own family was relatively small.

This must feel to Isaac like being thrown headfirst into a pond.

Cora managed to catch her mother's eye, and tilted her head slightly in Isaac's direction. Sara Lapp grasped the situation at a glance.

"Cora, why don't you and Isaac go out to the *grossdawdy haus,* for a while? No peeking inside, but the porch chairs are nice and comfortable."

Isaac rolled his eyes to his future mother in law with an almost comical look of relief, and Cora smiled.

"We don't want all these Lapps to scare Isaac away," Mrs. Lapp added primly, and lifted a glass of tea to her lips.

***

Cora grabbed the opportunity to get Isaac alone. She took his hand and led him out of the house and onto the front porch. It was a clear, moonlit night in late October. The stars shone with the crystalline brightness of crisp weather.

Isaac put his coat around Cora's shoulders, and she gave him a peck on the cheek. "I'm so proud of you, Isaac," she told him. "I would have thrown my hands in the air and run away screaming,"

"You have a *big f*amily," he admitted.

"Yes, but they're all going to adore you," she told him, leading the way down the front steps and out across her parent's lawn.

The *Lapp 'grandfather house' was a little distance beyond the main house. It was a small white cottage, ringed and mostly hidden by a thick, fragrant stand of cedar trees. It was close enough to be convenient, but far enough away to be private.*

"This is where my grandparents lived, when they were with us," Cora told him, climbing the cottage steps to the small front porch. Two big wicker chairs provided a tempting refuge, and Cora sank into one, and pulled Isaac down beside her. The sound of a creek burbled nearby in the darkness.

"This is our honeymoon cottage," she told him, proud that they had this place, this time.

"Honeymoon?" Isaac raised an eyebrow. "Are we Englisch now?"

"It's a blessing that we can do this, whatever name we call it by." Cora admonished him. Most Amish newlyweds went straight from marriage to visiting their families to their ordinary lives. "A gift for our wedding. They're getting it ready for us."

Isaac's hand reached for hers in the darkness. "It's a beautiful place," he said softly. "Quiet. Peaceful."

"It has a rock fireplace and big windows, too. Do you want to go inside and look?"

Isaac was thoughtful. "No," he replied at last. "Let's not spoil the surprise for them. Or for us."

Cora squeezed his hand. "Is that why you won't let me see your apartment yet?" she teased. "Is that a surprise, too?"

"Our house," he corrected her softly, and Cora could hear the smile in his voice. "Yes, I want it to be a surprise. I hope you'll like it."

Cora couldn't see his face in the darkness, and was glad of it, because she was seized by the temptation to go sit in his lap, again, and to ignore all protests.

"I know I will," she told him. "I'll be happy wherever you are, Isaac."

He didn't reply right away. The creek whispered somewhere out in the night, and the minutes passed.

"How do you feel about children, Cora?" he said at last.

"Children?" Cora stammered. "I know everybody expects us to have a lot, but I hadn't really thought about it. I mean, not yet, anyway. I want some, I guess -- one day."

"I'd like lots of children," Isaac murmured.

"Lots?"

"Yes. Four or five, maybe."

Cora dropped his hand. "Five?"

"Yes. Don't you want a big family?"

"Well, I –"

"I can see them in my mind," Isaac told her, and reached for her hand again. "Beautiful little girls, with your eyes. And strong boys, to work with me in the shop."

Cora's alarm melted. Oh, Isaac, she thought helplessly. You can make anything sound good.

"What do you think?"

"I – I guess," she told him. She glanced over to where he was sitting in the darkness. "You would make a wonderful father, Isaac," she said softly. "I guess it's only natural you for you to want lots of children."

"I want to give you a baby, Cora," he said softly. "It's the best gift of all. And I wouldn't mind if it happened right away."

In spite of her reservations, Cora couldn't help being swept up in the sweetness of that vision: Isaac's baby, in her arms.

"I have a good job, and I'm a hard worker," he went on. "And Hans Miller has promised me a promotion review soon. That will mean more money. Good money."

"Oh, Isaac, you don't have to –"

"It'll be enough for us to start a family, if we want."

"I'm not in any hurry, Isaac. And you don't have to worry about what you make. I don't care, really."

He didn't reply, as if he was thinking of something else. Finally he said:

"You're going to have a good life, Cora. I promise. We may not ever be rich, but you will never go without anything that you need. I swear it."

Cora sighed, shaking her head.

"Say something mean, Isaac. Really mean."

He turned toward her in the darkness, and she blurted:

"Because if you keep on being *so* adorable, and saying *such* sweet things to me, we're *both* going to end up surprised tonight!

"I'm just saying."

CHAPTER THREE

"Stand still, or you're going to get stuck!"

Cora knelt on the floor, pins in her mouth. She was fidgeting with the hem of Mary Stoltzfus' dress.

Mary sighed and her shoulders slumped. "How long do I have to stand here?" she complained.

"Until I can get the hem straight," Cora mumbled.

She was putting the finishing touches on her friends' dresses. As was custom, Cora had sewed not just her own wedding dress, but the dresses for the women in her wedding party -- her "side sitters."

They were all plain, serviceable Amish dresses, but Cora had made her own in a bright sky-blue.

"Here, let me do it." Katie Lapp braced herself on the bed and slowly lowered herself to a kneeling position.

"You're an angel, but you shouldn't, Katie," Cora objected. Her sister in law was glowing, beautiful, and vibrantly healthy. But she was pregnant, and clearly showing. It wouldn't be long now.

"There! How does that look?" Katie asked, tilting her head.

"It's perfect," Cora answered, and helped Katie to stand.

"Can I get out of this thing now?" Mary demanded.

"Yes, go ahead," Cora sighed. It looked like Mary was going to be the least girly of all her wedding attendants. Like all of them, Mary was staying at the Lapp house for the wedding; and Cora knew that as soon as she was free to go, Mary would disappear to some dark corner of the house and put her nose in a book. And not even a book about romance – something hideously boring, like *ancient poetry*.

Sure enough, as soon as Mary had pulled the dress off, and thrown on a tee and jeans, she was gone.

Katie watched her as she went. After the door closed, she gave Cora a wry smile. "Your new friend is a strange one," she observed.

"Yes," Cora sighed. "She's *never* going to get a man, behaving like she does."

"That would be a shame," Katie mused. "She isn't a bad-looking girl, if only she'd try."

"Hah!" Cora snorted, folding up Mary's dress, "you

should've seen her *before* I showed her how to fix her hair and wear makeup! She cared no more for her looks than a child. Even now, she only wears clothes to cover her nakedness."

"We're not *supposed* to wear makeup," Katie reminded her gently. "And there's nothing wrong with dressing plain."

Cora shook her head.

"Mary can't *afford* plain," was her frank assessment. "Mary is just on the *edge* of being pretty. She needs all the help she can get, to nudge her over."

A glint of mischief sparkled in her eye. "I may set her up at the wedding dinner. Who should I make her talk to?"

"Anybody but Hezekiah or Jeremy," Katie laughed. "They don't need broken hearts. I pity the boy who falls in love with that girl. She'll never look up from her books long enough to see him!"

But Cora put her finger to her lips. "There is *one* boy," she mused. "Do you know Seth Troyer?"

"I know the Troyer family," Katie replied, sitting down on the bed. "I was in school with his mother. She was much older, of course, but I remember her. She was a sweet girl."

"I've seen him hanging around her lately. He's a quiet thing, like her," Cora muttered. "Straight brown hair, pale and skinny! But he's *very* cute. Serious, too -- she might like that." Cora bit her thumb. "I think I'll throw them together at the wedding dinner. You never know what might happen."

"That's sweet of you, Cora." Katie put out her hand and pulled Cora down beside her. "But enough about your *friends*. Where's Isaac? I'm surprised he's not outside the door by now."

"Oh, he's out doing something mysterious," Cora told her. "He won't tell me, but I think he's working on the apartment. I don't expect him back until late. But I'm going to wait for him." She stopped, sighed.

"It's our last night before the wedding. I want to see him again before everything gets so busy."

Katie smiled. "Then you'd better show me your dress, now, before he comes back."

Cora dimpled and pulled a cardboard box out from underneath the bed. Inside was her wedding dress, folded carefully in tissue paper. There wasn't a scrap of lace or ribbon on it, but it was as blue as cornflowers -- blue as the sky.

"Oh, Cora, you did a beautiful job," Katie admired, smoothing her hand over the fabric. "Such tiny stitches! And all of them straight as a ruler."

She glanced at Cora affectionately. "This color is going to look lovely on you. It will match your eyes *exactly*. Darling, you're going to be a *breathtaking* bride."

Cora's eyes softened as she looked down at it. "When I see my dress, I know it's really happening. I'm marrying Isaac Muller! I still can't believe it," she replied softly. "It feels too good to be true."

Katie laughed. "Maybe to you," she told her sister in law. "But everyone else in town has been expecting it for years!"

Cora looked up, startled. "*Years*?"

"Of course," Katie giggled. "Darling, Isaac Muller has been crazy for you since he was a child. How could you *not* have known?"

"I don't know," Cora stuttered. "I just – I just didn't pay attention, I guess. And then I left."

"But now you're back," Katie reassured her, with a hug. "God was in that, Cora. He arranged it. And I'm so glad for your sake – and Isaac's." She giggled again. "And Joseph's! A merry chase the two of you have led him! Sometimes I thought he wasn't going to make it. Every time you sneaked outside to meet Isaac late at night, it was all I could do to keep Joseph from charging out after you with a pitchfork!"

Cora's mouth dropped open. "You *knew* about that?"

Katie nodded, laughing. "Of course we did! The two of you may as well have *painted a sign*."

"Oh, *Katie*," Cora gasped. She put a hand to her mouth. "Joes *knew*? And he didn't try to stop us? Oh -- you're right.

God was in it!”

Katie laughed. “It’s a miracle!”

CHAPTER FOUR

The house had been as busy as a hive of bees, but after midnight everyone had finally gone to bed, and it gradually became quiet. A white moon rode high in an indigo sky. It threw long blocks of white light across Cora's bedroom floor.

Her bedroom faced out over the front yard and the long driveway leading to the road. She sat at the window, keeping vigil for Isaac.

She saw him as soon as his buggy crested the long hill. Two tiny yellow lanterns bobbed in the distance, slowly becoming larger and brighter.

She pulled a shawl around her shoulders and padded out of her bedroom.

When she got down to the porch, she slipped quietly into the swing, waiting patiently for Isaac to pull the buggy to a stop, to finish unhooking the horse, and to lead it to the stable.

The light of the moon was almost bright enough to read by, and she could see him clearly as he came walking back. *Hear* him, too, with his big shoes.

When he came climbing wearily up the front steps, she simply held out her hand. He didn't seem surprised to see her sitting there. He came over and lay down on the swing, resting his head on her lap, and his feet on the slats of the seat.

She ran her fingers through his hair. "Tired?"

A groan was her only answer. She leaned down and kissed his forehead, and they were silent for a long time.

"You were out for a long time tonight," she said at last. "You must have been doing something important!"

"I was," he agreed, stretching.

"Tell me," Cora wheedled.

"Nope," he smiled.

"Were you at the apartment in town?"

"Maybe."

"Oh, Isaac, it isn't fair. Can't you give me even a *little* hint?"

"You'll see it soon."

Cora pinched him, and he wriggled and laughed, but

refused to budge. Cora laughed with him, but then fell silent.

"I still can't believe it's happening, Isaac," she murmured. "We're getting *married*!"

"Not backing out, are you?" Isaac teased her, squeezing her hand. "It took a long time for me to net you. I'd hate to show up for the wedding tomorrow, and find that you've changed your mind."

"Oh, *Isaac*," she sighed, "I won't change, if you won't. Promise me that we won't stop courting, just because we're married. Promise me you'll *always* be the same as you are now, *all* your life."

"Okay."

"I mean it. *Swear*. Because I want us to stay just like this. And some day, Isaac, if we argue, and you're angry, swear that you'll remember the way we are tonight, and love me again, like you do now. And I'll remember too, the way I love you. And then, even if we're *very* angry, we'll make up again."

"I won't be angry, Cora," he told her softly.

"*Promise*, Isaac," she pleaded.

"All right. I swear. I promise to stay the *same*," he said, solemnly. "Because I am your --"

He stopped, as if he couldn't bring himself to go on.

"Because I am a–"

"*Big, sweet marshmallow*!" Cora finished, and kissed him, laughing.

"And *you* -- promise you won't ever tell *anyone* else that you call me that, Cora," he admonished her, wagging a finger. "Can you hear the men in town talking? 'Here comes Isaac Muller -- the marshmallow!'"

Cora giggled, and kissed him, and they rocked back and forth for a while, drinking in the silence of deep night. Cora looked out across the dark fields, and murmured thoughtfully: "It's our last night, Isaac. I'm going to miss meeting you in secret, out under the stars."

"I won't," Isaac confessed. "It was always a long, *cold* walk back home."

Cora burst out laughing, and buried her mirth in Isaac's hair.

"I watched you, you know," she told him. "From my window. I watched you walk back across the fields, until I couldn't see you anymore. And I always imagined that the little yellow light I saw in the house at night was *your* window."

Isaac turned his head. "It was. How did you know?"

"I just *wanted* it to be. I sat there at the window and imagined you getting dressed for bed, and going to sleep."

"*Mmm*, it feels much better here, with you as my pillow. I could go to sleep right now," he yawned.

"I wish you could," she sighed. "I wish we could just be married *now*. It would be so much easier."

He didn't answer.

"Isaac."

He still didn't answer.

"Isaac."

Cora sighed, "Oh, *Isaac*," and then leaned down and kissed him gently. She sat there, guarding Isaac's sleep, stroking his shining hair until the moon rode on into the night sky and the night birds called out their soft, lovely songs.

CHAPTER FIVE

The next morning Cora stood in the huge Lapp living room, ramrod-straight, trembling in her black boots, her beautiful sky-blue dress and sheer, snowy apron.

It was happening at last.

She looked over at Isaac, so handsome in his black wedding suit, and hat, and bow tie.

Bishop Hottstetler was talking again, intoning words, but they were sliding over her like clear water rushing over stones. She grasped at them – these words about love, about commitment – but they fluttered away from her like birds, and were gone.

Now Isaac was looking at her. He squeezed her hand, nodded and said: *Yes*.

She drank up the light in his eyes, the look in them that promised her everything. He would never go back, she knew it: Isaac was as sure as the sunrise. He would be there for her until the day he died.

He had granted her wish again, in the daylight, in front of God and everybody.

He had given her the gift of an honorable man: he had *sworn.*

The bishop turned to her, asked her a question. She noticed every detail of the older man's face, his kind green eyes, the oddly curving lashes that ringed them. It was her turn to answer. There was only one word to say.

"*Yes.*"

Cora could hear someone sniffing softly in the background. The bishop read more words, and Isaac said *yes* again, and she said *yes*.

The bishop took Isaac's hand, and her hand, and joined them, and put his hand on top of them.

He was praying, and Cora bowed her head. The words were sliding away again, so she prayed a prayer of her own: *Oh Lord, thank you for giving me the sweetest man in the world. I'll be a good wife to Isaac – I promise.*

She looked up. The bishop was smiling at her.

It was done.

She was Isaac Muller's *wife*.

She turned to Isaac and smiled, and he held her hand so tight that it almost hurt, but she didn't let go. Everyone was around them, talking, laughing. Her mother came and kissed her, and she threw an arm around her neck. Her daed was shaking Isaac's hand, and Isaac's mother was reaching for her.

Then there was Joes, and she released Isaac's hand and went into his arms, laughing. She was thinking of how Katie had described him: poor Joes, running after them with a pitchfork!

"I'm so happy for you, sprout," he was saying, and it was true – she could see it in his eyes.

Then Katie was hugging her, and Isaac took her hand again, and they all went into the dining room, where the tables were all laid out and waiting.

***

It all seemed like a dream to Cora, a lovely dream: the smiling faces, the laughter, Isaac's hand clasping hers. They sat down at the bride's table, in the seats of honor, and people said things to her, and brought food, and they ate. There was so much of everything, all of it good, the crisp crunch of celery sweet against her tongue, but Cora barely ate – there was no need to eat. She was sure that she could live a thousand years on the love she felt in that room.

Her own happiness must be shining out of her eyes,

because she saw it reflected on the faces of her friends: in Katie, and Emma, and even Mary Stoltzfus, who had astounded her by sniffling and wiping her nose.

And most of all, from Isaac: She had never seen him so happy, so alive. His joy was deep, not always expressed in a smile, but she knew him. She could *feel* it. It radiated out of him like warmth from the earth.

She luxuriated in his joy like a soft fur coat. Isaac *loved* her, had *always* loved her, *would* always love her. She nestled into his chest, and he put his arm around her.

Then people came and cleared away the tables, and their friends and family brought all kinds of gifts: clocks and stoneware and sheets and pillows, quilts and kitchen utensils and little garden tools, seeds and churns and little handmade boxes, canned fruit and jam, and even -- a few books.

Mary Stoltzfus' doing, of course: Cora laughed inside, and knew she would never read them, but thanked Mary prettily, and looked around for Seth Troyer.

Sure enough, he was still there, loitering hopefully in the corner of the room. Cora leaned over and whispered to Katie. Her sister in law smiled, and nodded, and got up. Cora watched in amusement as Katie whispered to Mary, and then led her over to Seth. To Cora's delight, Mary looked at him, shrugged, and started to talk. Cora almost laughed out loud to see how Seth revived at this attention.

After the giving of gifts, there were games, and singing all afternoon. Cora drank it all in from her place on Isaac's chest, wishing with all her heart that it could go on forever.

By suppertime their guests had thinned to include mostly family and close friends. Mr. Muller and Cora's daed sat in honored places at the head of the table, and prayed, and they all ate, and laughed, and laughed again.

"Oh Lord," Cora's father prayed, "Please bless our children and keep them strong in You. Plant them in this place, and make them fruitful as a spreading vine. May they live under Your protection all their days, and thrive under Your love."

Amen, the table replied, and Isaac echoed: *Amen.*

Cora leaned on him, and closed her eyes, drinking in their voices, and the laughter, and the lovely warm glow that surrounded her like a quilt. She had never felt so loved in all her life, or so secure: her family was around her, Isaac's love was a shield between her and the world, and the love of God was radiant in her heart.

When I am sad or sick or old, Cora thought to herself, no matter what trouble ever comes to me in my life, I will remember this day.

And the joy of it will heal me.

CHAPTER SIX

"Well, here we are."

It was past midnight, the last guest had gone home, and Cora and Isaac were on their own – *at last.*

Isaac smiled at her, and pushed open the door of the little *grossdawdy* house. Golden light streamed out across their faces.

The interior was like a dollhouse. A crackling fire danced in the big stone fireplace, and two overstuffed chairs faced its light. There was a basket on the little table nearby. Cora could see a bottle of iced-tea, and fancy glasses, and what looked like chocolate and fruit.

"Oh, they must have worked all week," Cora breathed, following Isaac. "The place is *sparkling*. It looks new!"

Isaac took her hand. He flopped down into one of the big chairs, and pulled her down after him.

Cora landed in his lap, laughing, and tossed his hat across the floor. He looked up at her, smiling.

"Well, what *now*?" he teased.

She smiled, took his face in her hands, and promptly stopped his mouth. She had been starving for Isaac's lips, and nourished herself with their sweet, soft taste.

His arms closed around her, and she twisted into him. Her lips wandered over his mouth, down to his chin, along his jaw, and down to the firm skin of his neck. She let her lips linger on the pulse point, savoring the delicious warm *thrum* of his heart.

She pulled back to get her breath, and almost laughed aloud: Isaac's head was tilted back, and his blue eyes were on the ceiling. They had that dazed look that she loved, the one that made him look as if he'd been struck on the head with a skillet.

"Isaac, I want to see you without your shirt on," she whispered.

His eyes rolled down again to meet hers. He put his arms out wide in a gesture of surrender, and she unfastened the buttons of his shirt. "Do you know what I thought about in church every Sunday, Isaac?" she teased him, as she worked. "I sat there, wondering what you looked like *without your clothes on.*"

"Ach!" came his voice, but she saw his lips curve up.

Cora pulled his shirt open, pushed the suspenders off his shoulders -- and sat back in wonder, suddenly speechless.

He was *beautiful.*

His chest was broad as the side of a barn -- smooth, hard, and *perfect.*

Cora suddenly remembered the statues that she had seen in the museum in New York. Isaac's chest was *just like that*, and suddenly she understood their meaning: the statues were a celebration of *this* -- of youth and beauty and perfection.

Only the statues were cold and lifeless, and Isaac was warm and real. She put out her hand, and caressed his skin in wonder. It felt firm and smooth under her fingertips – there was solid muscle under it, firm and taut.

She untangled herself from his arms, stood up, and stepped back a few paces. She looked at him, serious now, and made a beckoning motion with her hands.

Isaac lifted himself from the chair, his eyes on hers. He slowly shed the rest of his clothes, still looking at her.

Cora let her eyes travel slowly down his body. Her mouth dropped open then formed one silent word:

"Wow."

Once, she had thought that Matt was handsome, but she had to say, Isaac Muller made him look like a little child.

When she looked up again, Isaac's expression told her that her awe must be obvious. His vulnerable look was now replaced by a wide smile.

Then he put out his hands, and beckoned gently in the air.

Cora felt her cheeks go blazing hot, and was surprised to feel a wave of shyness. She couldn't meet Isaac's eyes, but slowly unfastened the apron of her wedding dress and let it slide away. She pulled up the billowing skirt, stuck out a leg, rolled down the black stockings, and tossed them in his direction.

She mustered the courage to raise her eyes to his, and was surprised, not by the frying pan look, but something else, something different.

Isaac's eyes shone. He looked *overcome*.

Cora was seized by panic. He wasn't supposed to be *crying*! Was he *disappointed* by the way she looked?

Still, there was no backing out *now*.

Cora reached back and unfastened her dress. The dress slid off of her shoulders and fell into a bright heap on the floor. In a few quick movements, she came out of her undergarments.

She took a deep breath and looked up into Isaac's face. She had never felt so vulnerable in her life, and she could only pray that Isaac approved of her body as heartily as she approved of his.

But what she saw there assuaged her fears. Isaac's eyes glistened, but there was no mistaking the look in them. His eyes moved in wonder from her face, to her feet, and back again.

"Cora, you're so beautiful," he whispered. "*So* beautiful."

Cora went almost limp with relief. Then her confidence came surging back.

"Well are you going to do something about that, Isaac Muller, or are we going to wait *another* year?" she asked archly. "*Kiss* me!"

"*Yes, ma'am,*" Isaac replied, and reached for her.

***

Cora leaped into his arms and wrapped herself around him. His bare skin was firm and smooth and hot against hers, but his big hands on her were surprisingly gentle. Isaac caressed her lightly, almost reverently: her shoulders, her back, her waist, as if he was memorizing the feel of her body.

Then he reached under her suddenly and lifted her up into the air. Cora shrieked with laughter as he swung her around the little living room and carried her into the bedroom.

The bed was a beautiful antique, a colonial four-poster covered with a snow-white down coverlet. Another crackling fire murmured in a fireplace opposite the bed, but Cora only had a fleeting glimpse of these things before the coverlet pillowed all around her, and Isaac was lying by her side.

He leaned over to kiss her, and she reached up into his hair, tangling her fingers in it. His lips were still reverent, still gentle. He put his hand under her chin.

"Tonight is for you, Cora," he whispered. "I want you to tell me what feels good, what you want me to do."

She stopped kissing him to let it sink in: Isaac was giving her yet *another* unselfish gift.

She felt tears in her own eyes, and nodded. "All right, Isaac. I will." She took his face in her hands and smiled up at him.

"I want you make love to me, like a crazy man, *all night long*."

He looked down at her, grinned, and put two fingers to his temple in a fleeting salute.

CHAPTER SEVEN

"Don't open your eyes yet."

Cora stood perfectly still, holding her breath. Isaac was on the point of revealing their new apartment.

One of his hands covered her eyes, and the other fumbled with the doorknob. Their new home was a little two-story clapboard house on a street at the very edge of town. The house was owned by Isaac's employer. The lower floor was being used as a warehouse for company merchandise, but Isaac's boss, Hans Miller, had allowed Isaac to rent the apartment suite on the upper floor for the two of them to live in.

The bottom half of the house had not looked promising: the windows were dark and dusty and the front door was locked tight.

The only access to the second-story apartment was the small flight of stairs on the side of the building.

"Are you ready?"

Cora nodded.

"*Allll* right. Open your eyes!"

The door to their house swung back. Cora put her hands to her mouth. It was *beautiful.*

"Oh, Isaac!"

She stepped in, looking around, and her footsteps rang out on the wooden floor. The oak floorboards shone like silk, and the walls were a spotless white with bright blue trim around the doors and windows. The apartment looked just like an Amish house -- bright, airy and cheerful.

And instantly it was clear what Isaac had been doing during his mysterious absences: the apartment was *full* of his gorgeous, handmade furniture.

She turned to him. "You made all the furniture," she gasped. "It's *beautiful*! You must have been working for *months*!"

He looked down at her, and she could see that he was pleased by her joy. "More like a year," he admitted.

Cora walked across the floor, her eyes darting from piece to piece. A beautiful black oak grandfather clock ticked softly to itself on the far wall. The whitewashed brick fireplace was topped by a hand carved mantelpiece decorated with an oak tree design.

On one side of the room, a beautiful handmade rocker and side table flanked a small, spare day bed covered in a blue quilt.

"Oh, Isaac," she murmured, putting her hand to her mouth. She looked up at his smiling face, and without any further comment, threw herself into his arms.

Isaac laughed and spun her around in the air. "Are you ready to set up house with me, Cora Muller?" he teased her.

"Oh yes, Isaac," she replied -- but then frowned, and pulled back from him.

"Wait – you said you'd been working on these for a *year*?"

"Mmm."

"You must have been very sure I'd marry you! We were barely dating then."

"Oh, a man can tell," he deadpanned.

Cora put her hands on her hips, but couldn't keep from sputtering at his mock-innocent expression. "Well, I won't deny it," she giggled, "-- you *sexy* beast, Isaac!"

He flushed with pleasure like a child, and she couldn't resist reaching up to kiss his chin.

"I like it," he murmured, "*sexy beast*. It has a better ring than *marshmallow*."

***

He took her hand, and they explored the apartment together. It was fully furnished – all the furniture and lamps and even kitchen utensils were all there, all ready to be used.

There was a small propane stove in the kitchen, and a big wooden table ringed by handmade chairs. A pale blue, gas powered, refrigerator stood in the corner, and a tall wooden pie safe adorned one wall.

"Isaac, you shouldn't have done all this alone," she told him, squeezing his hand. "No wonder you were exhausted, poor darling! You should have waited and let me help you!"

"Oh, I had help," he admitted, "your mamm and daed, *and* mine, and your brother Joseph, and his children. Even that new friend of yours, the Stoltzfus girl."

Cora giggled. "What on earth did *Mary* do here?" she wondered aloud.

"Come and see," he invited, smiling.

Cora looked a question, and followed him to a small room at the back of the apartment. Isaac pushed the door open and stood aside.

Cora stood in the doorway, her eyes round. The little room was a tiny nursery, all set up for a future baby. Isaac had built a beautiful cherry wood crib and a matching rocker for her. And Mary – it must have been Mary – had sewn a quilt that almost covered one wall. It was a portrait in fabric of the little schoolhouse, and the oak tree nearby, and showed the children playing in the yard.

Cora put a hand to her throat, and shook her head. She couldn't speak.

"Someday we'll be using this room, Cora," Isaac told her softly, planting a kiss in her hair. "Maybe not long from now."

Cora nodded, overcome.

"Come and see the bedroom."

***

He led her around a corner and down the hall to a big room facing out over the back of the house. It was sunny, filled with light streaming in from a big picture window, and almost empty except for a magnificent cherry wood armoire and a huge cherry wood sleigh bed.

A gorgeous wedding ring quilt in blue and purple covered the bed, topped with white pillows. And just above the headboard was the tender inscription that Isaac had made and given to her as a wedding gift.

Isaac was looking at her, and Cora met his glance with swimming eyes.

"We can open this window," he told her, walking over to a big picture window. He unfastened the latch and threw it out, and fresh, cold air came pouring in. Cora walked over to join him, and looked down on a small yard with a big oak tree. "It'll be nice on the summer nights. Maybe it'll make it up to you for not meeting me outside," he teased.

"Oh, Isaac!" Cora sobbed, and went into his arms. He folded his arms around her and held her close.

"I take it that means you approve?" he teased.

She sobbed something unintelligible into his chest, and clung to him. He rocked her back and forth, smiled, and looked up at the ceiling.

CHAPTER EIGHT

"Marriage seems to agree with you," Mary Stoltzfus observed wryly.

On her first day back at school, the new Mrs. Isaac Muller was still in full newlywed flush. Cora was more beautiful than ever: her hair was like corn silk and her skin glowed. Her eyes were alive with happiness.

She had gone from working full time at the school, to working only a few days a week, but she looked glad to be back.

"Oh, Mary, the quilt was so beautiful!" Cora cried, and cast herself on Mary's neck. "It was so, *so* sweet of you!"

Mary endured her embrace in embarrassed silence, because they were in the schoolroom, and even though it was too early for the children, Mary was not an effusive girl.

"Yeah, okay," she mumbled. "I'm glad you liked it."

"I've missed being here," Cora told her softly. "I had a beautiful time at the cottage, and I couldn't be happier, but I still missed the children. <u>*And*</u> talking to you."

"That reminds me," Mary told her. "I have a bone to pick with you. I know you were the one who set that scrawny Seth Troyer onto me at the wedding. He babbled at me for *thirty* minutes! And now he follows me around like a puppy dog. You *owe* me."

Cora laughed delightedly. "I knew it! He *likes* you."

"He's a pain in the butt! I don't have time for him."

"Why not?" Cora cried. "He's as cute as can be! And what's so important that you can't make a few minutes for a handsome boy?"

Mary looked down at the floor, and mumbled a few muffled words.

Cora smiled knowingly. "*I* know what's wrong. You haven't ever kissed a boy before, have you?"

Mary gaped at her.

"*Mmm-hmm*! I thought so! It's normal to be a little nervous at first, but once you start, you never look back. Why don't you try with Seth? He won't mind, he likes you."

"I'm not going to –"

"Be sure to wear English clothes and makeup when you

see him," Cora urged her. "They look so good on you. You're still on your rumspringa, you can get away with it."

"I *will,*" Mary told her, "but I'm doing it because I *want* to – not because I'm trying to snare Seth Troyer. I have plans. I want a career!"

Cora set her mouth firmly. "Mary Stoltzfus, you're *never* going to get married, if you take that attitude. What good is a career if it keeps you from meeting boys? You should throw all those boring books out the window -- they're *ruining* your life! But don't worry, *I'll help you.*"

Cora squeezed Mary's hand encouragingly then looked around them. When she saw they were alone, she whispered:

"*I have a cell phone.* I'll write down my number for you." She took a pencil and scrawled hastily on a scrap of paper.

"Call me. I can walk you through everything. I can tell you *just* what to say and do when Seth comes around."

Mary sat up in alarm. "Wait – *when* he comes around? *What have you done?*"

Cora dimpled and refused to answer, and Mary's mother walked in, putting an end to the conversation.

Cora pressed the phone number into her hand, and Mary quickly hid the scrap of paper inside one of her books.

Because if anyone else saw it, they were both in trouble. The elders considered cell phones an undesirable influence, and they were strictly forbidden under the *Ordnung*.

The school bell mercifully cut their conversation short, and Mary retreated gratefully to the familiar routine of preparing for the school day. It was far less challenging that being tempted with a cell phone, or devilled with that silly puppy, Seth Troyer.

And when the children started to arrive, their joy at Cora's return pulled Mary's attention to safer topics.

But even so, that little scrap of paper nagged at her all through the school day, like a persistent whisper.

***

When she got home that afternoon, Mary went up to her room and sat down on the bed. She pulled Cora's guilty note out of her book.

She looked down at it. If she was honest with herself, she *had* thought about getting a cell phone, but had never dared to buy one.

Only *Cora* would dare.

But if Cora got caught, she'd be hauled up before the elders, get a long lecture about separation from the world, and then be put on warning. Her husband and her whole family would be disgraced.

If she was caught with a phone a *second* time, she might

even be shunned. *That* possibility was terrifying – no one could speak to her, or acknowledge her in any way, until she repented.

Mary tilted her head, wondering if Cora's new husband had given her the phone. Knowing her friend, Mary judged it more likely that he didn't know a *thing* about it.

Mary bit her lip. Cora was taking a terrible risk, and in the most careless way imaginable. She was a teacher, and if anybody found out that she was defying the *Ordnung*, she wouldn't be one anymore.

Of course, Mary acknowledged, if she got one *herself*, things might not go so well for her, either. Even though she hadn't yet joined the church, she was still a teacher at the school, and could ill afford a scandal.

Still, she had to admit that she *did* want a phone.

Having one would be a great convenience -- *if* nobody found out. It would make it much easier to pitch story ideas to publications, to find a new job, to order pretty clothes, to –

She stopped herself, hardly daring to articulate it, even to herself.

It would make it easier for her to *live like the English.* Like the people in New York. Or *Paris*.

Mary flopped over on her elbows and closed her eyes, imagining Paris, and wishing that she would win that French essay contest, so she could travel there.

Of course, just finding the courage to mail off her entry was a miracle in itself – even if she hadn't heard a word back from them. Even if she probably *never* would.

It made her feel almost like a writer. And at least it gave her something to dream about.

But her daydream was short-lived. Her fantasy was rudely interrupted when her mother's voice came drifting up from below.

"Mary, come down! You've got a visitor!"

Mary rolled over on her back and put her hands over her eyes. *Oh, no.*

"Who is it?" Mary called, but she already knew the answer.

Her mother's voice was jumping with excitement. "It's *Seth Troyer*! Don't keep him waiting, Mary – come down and say hello!"

The devil, Mary groaned irritably, and pulled herself off of the bed. She stuck the little scrap of paper down between the mattresses, and dragged herself downstairs, promising herself that she would push Seth Troyer down an embankment if she could lure him far enough away from the house.

And read Cora Muller the *lecture of her life*, tomorrow at school.

CHAPTER NINE

"Hello -- *Mary*."

Seth Troyer was sitting primly on their living room sofa, and smiled up at her as she descended the stairs.

Mary felt her mouth dropping open. He was wearing big, round, black glasses. He looked like a panda.

"Do you wear glasses now, Seth?" she blurted, fighting the urge to burst out laughing.

He lowered his eyes and smiled demurely. "It must be all the *books* I'm reading," he confided. "It kind of strains the eyes, but it's worth it, don't you think?"

Mary stared at him, speechless.

"Mary, why don't you offer our guest some *refreshments*?" her mother urged, giving her a significant look.

"Um – what – what would you like, Seth?" Mary said faintly, taking care not to make direct eye contact.

"Oh, anything *you* made would be good, I'm sure," he told her, smiling.

"That's very sweet of you, Seth," her mother smiled, and grabbed her by the arm.

Once Mary's mother had pulled her into the kitchen, she rounded on her.

"Mary Stoltzfus, you have the most shocking manners I've ever seen in my life," she hissed. "That poor boy is *interested* in you, and if you had any sense at all, you'd welcome him!"

"Oh, this is Cora Muller's doing," Mary complained, shrugging. "She set this little tadpole on me, and now I can't get rid of him!"

"Cora is your friend, and you should be grateful for her kindness!" Fannie Stoltzfus retorted. "Now you are going to go *back* in there, and *smile*, and be a good hostess to that boy, because if I catch you making that awful face where he can see it, I'll wear you within an inch of your life -- sixteen or *no*!"

She pressed a plate of cookies into Mary's hands, and pushed her back through the door.

Mary stumbled into the room, righted herself, and suppressed a sigh. She walked over to Seth and pushed the plate of cookies at him.

"Hungry?" she asked tonelessly.

"Don't mind if I do," Seth answered, taking a handful. "*Mmm*, good!"

Mary looked over at the kitchen door. Her mother was still there, watching her grimly.

She pinched her lips together then brightened. "Seth, how would you like to see the garden?" she asked. "I just *love* flowers, and some of them are beginning to come in."

Seth sat up straight. "I'd love to!"

"We could talk there," Mary smiled, taking him by the arm. "We won't go far, of course," she added, as an aside to her mother, "but it *is* awkward to have a *chaperone*."

Fannie Stoltzfus frowned, and narrowed her eyes.

"We can discuss books, and – *stuff*."

Seth Troyer giggled like a girl and took her arm. Mary pulled her lips into a smile and led him past her ominously silent parent, out through the living room, and into the front yard.

They walked down the garden path, and Mary was careful to maintain a placid face as long as they were within sight of the house. But as soon as they had rounded the corner and were shielded by bushes, she grabbed Seth's arm and hissed:

"Now *listen to me*, you little worm. I don't know why you came over here, but I'm *not interested* in making out with you. I just want to be left alone!"

Seth nodded knowingly. "Yes, she *said* that you'd say that -- at first."

"*She*?"

"Cora Muller. She explained *everything*. Don't worry, *I* understand." He reached out and took her hand reassuringly.

Mary shook it away. "I don't care what she told you. She's a meddling pain, and just *wait* until I get ahold of –"

There was a muted buzzing from somewhere in Seth's hat. "Oh, I'm sorry, Mary – I'm getting a call."

Mary froze mid-tirade, thunderstruck.

"*You* have a cell phone?"

Seth reached into his hat and pulled out a phone. "*Hello*? Yes. Look, I can't talk right now. I'm in the middle of something *important*." He smiled at Mary apologetically. "Yes, that's right. I'll have to get back to you. Later, bye."

Mary put her hands on her hips. She looked down at her feet, and then off to one side, and then up at the sky, and then back at Seth Troyer's face.

She squeezed her eyes together, and forced her lips to form the question: "How – how many *other* people do you know who have cell phones, Seth?"

He tucked the phone back into his hat. "Oh, a few. The ones who are – well, *you* know! But back to our conversation. I *understand* that you might be nervous about seeing a man of the world alone," he told her earnestly. "But I didn't come here to take advantage of your innocence."

Mary stared at him grimly. Her eyes moved to the edge of the garden, where the ground fell steeply away to a pond.

"I just wanted to get to know you better," he added, and took off the bulky glasses. "I think we might be *great* friends."

Seth turned his eyes on her in what she imagined was his best imitation of a puppy-dog look. And actually, now that she saw him up close, Mary had to admit that he *did* have rather nice eyes: they were ringed in thick, dark lashes and were a dark, vibrant green.

He had nice hair, too: it was a rich chestnut brown, and shone in the sun.

But of course, none of those good points could make up for him being a *puppy*, a *tadpole*, a total *worm*.

Mary did some quick calculations in her head, and decided to change her tack. She replied smoothly:

"Oh. Well, *that's* different, Seth. I'm glad you want to be friends. Let's be friends, *yes*.

"Because you must understand, I will probably *never* marry. I don't want to mislead you, it isn't fair." She leaned toward him, and added, in a hushed voice: "You see, I – I can *never* have children." She bowed her head.

Seth's mouth dropped open. "*Oh.*"

"Even my friend Cora doesn't know," she added, taking his arm. "So you see, *naturally* I don't like to lead boys on. It would only lead to heartache."

"Oh, *Mary.*"

"Yes. I'm resigned."

Seth patted her on the back in awe. "You're so *brave*, Mary."

"I know."

"Well, I – I don't know what to say," Seth stammered.

"It's very awkward, I know, but it's best to get it right out into the open. But there's no reason we can't *still* have a happy time. Now that you've come all the way over here, Seth, it would be shame to waste the afternoon. Would you like to come inside and play checkers?" she asked sweetly.

Seth threw her a sickly smile and shook his head. "I – I guess another time."

"I understand."

She walked him back to the front of the house, and shook

his hand, and waved. He trudged off without even the pretense of a graceful exit, with his shoulders slumped and his head down, and slowly disappeared down the road outside.

Mary put her hands on her hips and enjoyed a long, evil belly laugh before turning to the house.

But to her surprise, her mother was standing *right* behind her.

"*What* did you say to that boy?" she demanded. "He looked like he'd been dunked in ice water!"

"I just told him we could be *friends*," Mary replied innocently, and returned to the house with the wounded air of one who had been unjustly accused.

CHAPTER TEN

After long deliberation, Mary decided *not* to murder Cora Muller.

But she was determined to throw her off the trail, and decided that the best way to do that was to *pretend* that her matchmaking had been a success. Then, hopefully, Cora would forget all about setting her up with Seth Troyer, and move on to a *new* victim.

Accordingly, she arrived at the schoolroom bright and early the next morning. And when Cora walked through the door, Mary was ready for her.

"Well, don't *you* look bright and shiny this morning!" Cora exclaimed in delight.

Mary had pinched her cheeks rosy, and they glowed. She smiled primly, and dug into the floor with the toe of one shoe.

"Did something *good* happen?" Cora prodded, in a

meaningful tone.

Mary shook her head, and looked out of the window, and smiled.

"Something *did* happen!" Cora exclaimed. "Tell me!"

Mary shrugged, and tried to blush. "Oh, nothing important. That worm, Seth Troyer, came over to the house yesterday – that's all."

"Seth Troyer came over to see you? Oh, Mary, how *exciting*!"

Mary dropped her eyes bashfully.

"I *told* you he likes you. Lucky you, to have such a cute boy on your string!"

Mary almost giggled, but decided not to push her credibility.

"Well, I have to admit, he's *almost* acceptable," she confided. "In a scrawny kind of way."

"Oh, Mary, you and your sense of humor," Cora chided her, smiling. "I'm so glad you *finally* recognize that Seth Troyer is a little hunk. Some other girl will snap him up, if you don't."

"Oh, I *know*."

Cora reached over and hugged her, laughing. As she did so, her purse spilled open and a sheaf of letters and circulars fell out.

"Oh, no," Cora fretted, gathering them up quickly, "I just grabbed the mail on the way out this morning. Can't let anybody see *this* one!" She pulled a shiny mail order catalog out of the pile.

"I only order lingerie out of it," she confided. "But the clothes are so cute, I can't help looking at them." She opened the pages, riffling through the sections.

Mary sat up straight, and forgot about pretending to be excited about Seth Troyer. Cora was doing something *much* more interesting.

She was crowding the fence -- *again.*

"Wait a minute, go back." Mary pointed to a page in the dress section. "Oh – look at that one. That's *really* pretty."

It was a simple, hip-hugging navy dress with a striped top over a solid skirt.

"That would be so cute on you for spring," Cora agreed. "It looks kind of French."

Mary tilted her head. "*Yes* – now that you mention it." She couldn't help imagining herself in it, now that Cora had put the idea into her head.

"Ooh – look at this little red number," Cora pointed out. "Such a great color, it looks wonderful on every skin type," she sighed. "Oh, I *wish* I could – but no, I promised my husband," she smiled.

She flipped a page. "And these are the *shoes*," she groaned. "This little strappy thing would be perfect with the navy dress. *Such* a sophisticated look!"

Mary grabbed the catalog and flipped it over. "What store is this?"

"Oh, it's one of those mail-order stores," Cora grimaced. "It's so inconvenient to *mail* in an order, filling out *paper forms* is such a pain, but that's what we *have* to do, I guess."

She looked up suddenly.

"Quick, Mary, get rid of it – here comes your mother!"

Mary shoved the catalog under a bench lid and sat on it. Cora adjusted her bonnet primly.

Fannie Stoltzfus walked in, to be greeted by two innocent, upturned faces.

"Good morning, girls."

"Good morning," Cora beamed.

"*Good morning*, mother," Mary sang.

The older woman's eyes narrowed. She shot her daughter a look that said, *I'm watching you.*

And as soon as her back was turned, Mary grabbed under the bench lid and stuffed the catalog into her *own* bag.

Her mother started talking to the students, and the school day started, but Mary's mind wasn't on it. She went through the motions of going over lessons, of answering the children's questions, of supervising projects, but she was sleepwalking.

Because in her mind, she was strolling down the *Avenue des Champs-Élysées* in Paris, wearing a chic navy dress and strappy sandals.

CHAPTER ELEVEN

That evening Cora stood at the window on tiptoe, peeking down into the front yard. It was almost time for Isaac to get home from work, but there was no sign of him yet in the street below.

The coast was clear.

Cora reached into her purse, pulled out her secret cell phone, and punched in a number.

"Hello, Seth? It's Cora Muller. Yes! So tell me -- *how did it go*?

"Well, I *warned* you that she'd be a tough one.

"You what? Oh, I *wish* you hadn't worn the glasses, but that's all right.

"Did you show her the phone, like I told you? *Good.*

"What? Oh, Seth!" Cora burst out laughing, and clapped a

hand over her mouth.

“She’s trying to play us. No. *No*.

“I promise you, Seth, she *can*. Yes, that was just a – well, Mary can be a little mean at first, but she’s a *very* sweet girl, once she trusts you.

“Don’t worry about that. I’m going to try something new. It may not work, but it doesn’t, we’ll try something else.

“The cell phone is important. Keep showing her the cell phone.

“*No*, for heaven’s sake! You don’t want anybody else to see it!”

The sound of Isaac’s footsteps on the landing outside brought her head up sharply.

“Seth, I have to go. Yes, I’m working on it, I promise! She’s going to fight like a wildcat, but we’ll get her!

“If my plan works, she’ll be talking to you soon. And when you see her, Seth, talk about everything English. She *loves* English things -- especially if they come from *France*.”

Cora hung up, and quickly tucked the cell phone behind a little false wall in her purse. And not a moment too soon -- Isaac came walking in while she still had her hand on the bag.

“The sexy beast is *home*,” he announced, smiling, and Cora ran over and threw her arms around him.

Isaac's breath moved her hair. "Did you *say* something while I was coming in, Cora?"

Cora shook her head.

"Crazy," he shrugged. "I thought I heard your voice."

"Oh, silly *Isaac*." Cora stood on tiptoe and gave him a reassuring peck on the lips.

Isaac received the kiss, but apparently thought the taste of it was a little odd. He pulled back, looked down at her -- and looked again. His brows moved together in a faint frown.

The worried expression that dawned across his face reminded Cora powerfully of Joes.

"Is -- something going on, Cora?"

"Nothing," she chirped. "Wash up and come to dinner."

He didn't reply, but gave her a long, puzzled look as he put his lunch pail down on the table, and rolled up his sleeves, and crossed the room.

***

Dinner that night was almost spartan by their usual standards: Cora had only had time to make a macaroni and cheese casserole, and a broiled chicken, and some biscuits and green beans and corn on the cob. She had it all laid out on the kitchen table when Isaac returned.

He sat down at the table with a huge, satisfied sigh. "I've been looking forward to this for *hours*," he confessed, rubbing his hands.

Cora was standing behind him, and began to massage his shoulder muscles with her fingers.

"Poor Isaac, you're working too hard," she frowned. "Your shoulders are all knotted up. How does *this* feel?" she smiled.

"*Ohhh*, yeah," he groaned. He closed his eyes, and his head swayed gently to the rhythm of her hands. "*Mmmmm.* Right *there* – and a little to the left."

"Do you *have* to work overtime, Isaac?" she pressed. "The extra money isn't that important. We're still *newlyweds,* after all."

He opened his eyes and grinned up at her. "Did you miss me?"

For answer, Cora leaned down and kissed him just under his ear, and then nipped the lobe with her teeth.

"*Ach*! Don't you have any pity!" he yelped, raising a hand to his ear. "Is that any way to treat your husband?"

"*How would you like to be treated, Isaac*?" she whispered, and nipped him again.

He put an arm around her and pulled her down on the bench beside him. "Now sit – *sit down*, I tell you, and behave like a civilized woman, so we can eat our food."

Cora crawled up into his lap, and put herself bodily between him and the table. “Are you telling me, Isaac Muller, that I come in *second*, behind your *dinner*?” She tangled him all up in her arms.

“Now, now, *Cora*, I’m starving,” Isaac pleaded, reaching for a biscuit over her shoulder. “I’ve been working nonstop since six o’clock this morning and I only had – only had a little sandwich –”

“You don’t *love* me anymore,” she murmured, kissing his neck.

“I never said that, I just want my dinner –”

“Instead of me.”

Isaac sighed, sensing defeat, and cast a longing glance at the chicken. He reached for a handful of biscuits, wrapped them up in a napkin, and allowed himself to be pulled to his feet, and led off down the hall.

***

An hour later, Isaac stared up at the ceiling of their bedroom and munched a buttered biscuit.

“Well, you shouldn’t tease me,” Cora was saying. “You *did* say that the sexy beast was home. What is that *supposed* to mean?”

“It means I’ll have to be more careful what I say,” Isaac

mumbled, licking butter off his fingers.

Cora caressed his shoulders. "Well, your *muscles* are all relaxed now," she smiled.

He sputtered and grinned at her, with his cheeks full of bread. Cora giggled and kissed him.

"My sweet Isaac! I'll serve the rest of your dinner here in bed." She threw off the sheet and disappeared down the hall, wearing nothing but a smile.

Isaac leaned out over the edge of the bed and called after her, "Stay away from the windows, Cora -- remember that this is a *tourist town*!"

CHAPTER TWELVE

It was past midnight, and the only sounds in Katie Lapp's bedroom were the soft snoring of her husband Joseph, and the occasional murmur of an owl from somewhere in the fields outside their farmhouse.

But Katie lay awake in bed, staring at the ceiling.

She frowned and pressed her hand to her stomach. She had been having ever-increasing pains for most of the day, but she had said nothing. She had been through one false start in the last few weeks, and she hadn't wanted to trouble Joseph again for a false alarm.

But her pain was quickly building to a point where she could no longer hide it.

"*Oh*!"

She clutched her stomach, wincing.

"Oh, heaven help me," she whispered, and then her eyes

flew open wide.

It wasn't a false alarm this time.

"Joseph – Joseph, *wake up*."

Her husband didn't reply.

"Joseph!" She reached over and shook him.

"What? What?" he mumbled, sitting up. "Is something wrong?"

"Send for the midwife!"

Joseph cracked a nervous smile, and scrambled out of bed. "I'll call her. Don't worry. Do you need anything?"

Katie shook her head. "Just call Jenny."

Joseph reached under the bed and pulled out the cell phone. Katie looked over at him and frowned.

"What have you got there?" she murmured. "Joseph, *that's a* –"

"Hello? Is this Jenny? This is Joseph Lapp.

"Yes -- it's the real thing this time. Can you come over?

"Thank you, Jenny. Yes, of course. *Hurry*!"

He hung up, but Katie's eyes were still on the phone. She shook her head. "Joseph, please throw it away. We can't have a cell phone in this house. It's against the *Ordnung*. I won't have the children seeing it."

"They won't see it," he assured her. He sat down on the bed next to her and took her hand.

"I love you, Katie," he said softly.

"Now you're trying to get around me," she told him, and his smile broadened. He leaned down and kissed her, and she couldn't restrain a weak smile in answer.

But the pain returned again with new ferocity. Katie gasped, arched her back, and writhed away from him.

"*Oh*!"

She squeezed her eyes shut and clenched the pillow until the wave passed. When she opened her eyes, she felt almost sorry for Joseph, to see the look of anguish on his face.

"It will be all right, Joseph," she told him.

He caressed her cheek. "I feel so helpless," he whispered. "I wish I could take the pain for you."

"It will be all right. Just think, Joseph – it won't be long now. *Our* baby."

"No, little *mamm*," he replied tenderly, brushing a wisp of hair back from her face.

***

Jenny Stephens was an English midwife who had 15 years

of house calls under her belt. She was a tiny woman, barely five feet tall, and had short, curly red hair and round wire glasses.

Her car pulled up outside about an hour later. She and her assistant, an Amish girl named Sarah, unpacked the car like soldiers setting up in the field. They marched into the house without more than a cursory knock, set their kit out on the kitchen table, and began to carry pieces of it upstairs.

Joseph greeted them at the bedroom door. “Come in.”

Jenny set the birth bag down on a table and went over to Katie, who was silent, but moving her legs restlessly.

“How’re you doing, Katie?” she asked. Her assistant came over and slipped a blood pressure cuff over Katie’s arm.

Katie lifted her eyes to Jenny’s face and gave her a strained smile.

“Let me check you.” She moved to the foot of the bed. “You’ve been holding out on us, Katie -- you’re *very* dilated! Can you sit up? It might help you along.”

Joseph moved to help Katie sit upright, but her head rolled back on her shoulders, and she squeezed her eyes shut, suppressing a moan.

“Try to rest between contractions,” Jenny said brightly. “It might help with the pain to think about something calming.”

Katie nodded, and closed her eyes. Her lips moved

soundlessly. Joseph took her hand and massaged it, following her silent prayer with quiet words of his own.

Katie squeezed her eyes tight, fighting a wave of pain, and gripped Joseph's hand hard.

"The Lord is my light...."

Another contraction, another wave of pain.

"And my salvation." She opened her eyes, looked up at Joseph's face. His eyes were on her, warm and loving.

"The Lord is the stronghold...." She arched her back and her chin tilted up to the ceiling.

"Of my life."

"Would you like some pain medication?" Jenny asked.

Katie shook her head. She closed her eyes, retreating within herself to a place containing only her, and the pain, and the darkness. Even the grip of Joseph's hand seemed to fade away.

The waves were like colors in her mind: red, and orange, and yellow, and each one stronger than the last. The pain built and built and built until she was doubled up; it then crested, and fell away, and slowly built again.

Jenny's voice, and Joseph's, and the sound of the women moving around her, all faded to a faint buzzing.

"The Lord is my light..."

A wave of red wracked her body.

"And my salvation."

The wave deepened to purple, and she almost cried aloud.

"The Lord is the stronghold…."

The wave fell away sharply, and she went limp.

"Of my life."

The wave built again, and a sweet, piping voice came laughing out of the shadows.

"A sister -- a sister, Mamm!"

Jenny's urgent voice broke through the darkness and the pain.

"Push, Katie, push hard!"

Katie set her jaw and pushed with all her might, and Jenny's joyous voice broke through the darkness.

"Congratulations – it's a little girl!"

Katie opened her eyes and looked at Joseph. He squeezed her hand, and kissed it. His long, beautiful eyelashes were clumped together and wet.

"Our baby. *Our* baby girl, Kate," he whispered -- and then smiled.

CHAPTER THIRTEEN

"Hello, Dorathea. Hello, *hello* there."

By midmorning of the next day, Katie's mother had arrived. She laughed and rocked the baby back and forth in her arms.

Dorathea was a beautiful child, pink and perfect and dainty. Katie's eyes moved hungrily over the curve of her baby's cheek, of the peach down of her new skin. Her little mouth was like a tiny pink rosebud, and her lashes were long and dark, just like Joseph's. In her baby bonnet and perfect blue gown, Dorathea looked more like a doll than a real child.

"Drink up now." Joseph's soft voice was warm in her ear. He pressed a cup of herbal tea into her fingers. Katie smiled up at him gratefully and sipped dutifully from the cup. Ever since Dorathea's birth, Joseph had coddled and spoiled her in the most delightful way imaginable.

Katie took another sip of tea. She should feel guilty, but she didn't. It was *wonderful*.

There was a soft tapping at the door, and it opened to reveal the children. Caleb was poised on the threshold, his head tilted to one side like a curious bird.

"Come in and see your little sister, Caleb," Joseph encouraged him.

Caleb ventured in shyly, his big eyes on the baby. Emma and the boys crowded behind him.

"Isn't she perfect?" Mary Lapp beamed.

"What's her name?" Caleb asked.

"*Dorathea*," Mary told him.

She leaned down and let Caleb look at his little sister's pink, sleeping face. His blue eyes were round with wonder.

Hezekiah and Jeremy hung back, but were frankly curious, craning their necks to get a peek of the baby's face under her tiny bonnet.

"Can I hold her?" Emma asked shyly.

Mary Lapp smiled and carefully transferred the baby to her arms. Emma took her tiny, squirming sister and smiled down into her face.

"She's *beautiful*," Emma murmured, and rocked her back and forth in delight.

Katie watched the children's reception of the baby with an overflowing heart, but when she turned to Joseph she was surprised to see an odd look on his face. His eyes were not on Dorathea, but on Emma, watching how she held the baby, how she cooed and laughed.

Joseph's eyes held joy, but a joy mingled with something else as well. Something wistful and almost sad.

She reached up and squeezed his hand.

He smiled, and nodded slightly, but his glance returned to Emma – to her shining eyes, and her laughing nonsense words to the baby.

"You're just a tiny little baby, Dorathea – yes, you *are*."

***

That evening, after the children had gone to bed, Katie cradled Dorathea in her arms. She stroked the baby's cheek. It was pink and petal-soft and perfect.

She looked up at Joseph through shining eyes.

"Thank you," she told him quietly. "I wanted her so badly. Thank you for giving her to me."

He sat down on the edge of the bed and cupped the baby's head in his hand.

"She's so beautiful," he murmured. "Like her mother."

Katie smiled, and then shook her head. "It shouldn't please me when you say such things, Joseph Lapp. But it always does."

He leaned down to kiss her, and then stood up again. "We're going to need help when your mother goes back home. What do you think about Cora coming over for a few days to help Emma?"

"Isaac might have something to say about that. Who would take care of him?"

Joseph shrugged. His tone was noncommittal. "What if he agreed?"

Katie looked up at him with dawning comprehension.

"You've already *asked* them, haven't you?"

"I never asked. Cora volunteered."

Katie's eyes widened. "You *called* them on that cell phone!"

Joseph nodded.

"*Cora* has a cell phone, too! --*You gave it to her* -- didn't you, Joseph?" she gasped.

"Now, Katie, you need to rest –"

"Does *Isaac* know about this?"

"I don't know."

"He'll be furious! Oh, Joseph, what if someone *else* finds out?"

"There are more things to consider than just getting caught."

"Yes – like the *Ordnung*!"

"It's about *safety*, Kate. What if Cora had a cell phone when she was running from that monster?" Joseph replied quietly.

Katie looked down at the baby. "There's no monster any more, Joseph."

"No, thank God. But he's not the only one in the world."

"She doesn't need a cell phone *here,* Joseph. And neither do we."

Joseph's eyes moved to the baby. He said nothing, but Katie flushed a bright red and looked away.

"If you think the elders should change the *Ordnung*, maybe you should suggest a change," she said at last. "But to defy the *Ordnung* without asking –"

"The *Ordnung* changes very slowly, if it changes at all," he replied. "You know that."

"We promised."

"I've made a decision, Kate," he said softly.

She bit her lip and nodded. But she added quietly: "Then don't let the children see it." She lifted her eyes to his.

"And I'm *trusting* that you won't give them cell phones of their own, Joseph," she added.

He didn't reply, but held out his arms for the baby. Katie lifted Dorathea gently from her breast and gave her wriggling daughter into Joseph's hands.

But as he put the baby down into her crib, she couldn't resist adding: "I know now why Cora is your favorite, Joseph Lapp," she sighed. "You aren't as different as you like to think. You love her because she does the things you *want* to, and never have. Until now!"

CHAPTER FOURTEEN

"She looks *just like you*, Katie," Cora marveled.

Cora was holding Dorathea, rocking her back and forth. She looked up and laughed. "But you're right, she *does* have Joe's lashes. I was always jealous because Joe's lashes were longer than mine. They've always been as long as a girl's!"

"Joseph does have beautiful eyes," Katie agreed. "It was the first thing I noticed about him."

"Don't you tell him so. We have to keep him humble."

Katie looked at her sister-in-law with gratitude. "Thank you for coming over, Cora. It was sweet of you. Emma manages very well, but an extra pair of hands is so welcome."

"Oh, you know I always love to come here," Cora answered lightly. "I might even sneak away with Isaac for a while, for old time's sake. But it won't be as much fun now that everybody *knows* about it."

Katie laughed in spite of herself. "You're impossible, Cora. Where *is* Isaac?"

"Oh, he's downstairs talking to Joes about crop rotation, or something like that. I had to leave, I was falling asleep."

She leaned down and gave Dorathea a butterfly kiss.

"Do you mind if I take her downstairs? I want to show her to Isaac."

Katie reached up and caressed the top of Dorathea's little bonnet wistfully. "Yes, it's all right."

Cora laughed at her expression. "Don't worry, mamm. I promise I'll bring her right back." Cora tickled the baby's chin. "Won't I, sweet girl? *Yes*."

She winked at Katie and carried Dorathea down the hall and down the stairs to the living room.

She had expected Joes and Isaac to be in deep conversation, but to her surprise, Dorathea's arrival overwhelmed the crops, the economy, local business, and even the neighborhood news.

She held Dorathea up to them to see, smiling. "Look, Isaac!" she dimpled, "Isn't she *adorable*?"

They both stood up as she entered. Joseph couldn't resist coming over to kiss the baby, and to play with her fingers.

Cora laughed at him. "Joes, you should see yourself," she

teased him.

"I can't help it," he admitted, and took Dorathea in his arms. "Every time is like the first time."

He held the baby up to his cheek, and kissed her ear.

"Papa Joes," Cora laughed, and turned to Isaac. She was going to say something, but Isaac's expression stopped her.

He was looking at Dorathea with a kind of sad longing in his face. He was smiling, happy for Joes, but it was crystal clear to Cora that seeing Joes playing with Dorathea was bittersweet for Isaac.

His longing for a child was stamped on his face so plainly that Cora was glad that there was no other woman in the room.

She would have read it off him like print.

Cora looked down, feeling suddenly guilty for showing off the baby. She hadn't realized until now that Isaac might feel – not envy, but –

"Would you like to hold her, Isaac?" Joes was asking.

Isaac smiled crookedly, and held out his big hands. Joes put the baby carefully into them, and Isaac's eyes lit up from within with such a sweet pleasure that Cora couldn't take her eyes off his face.

It was impossible not to see him as a father, to imagine him with their own baby in his arms.

He was looking down into Dorathea's face with so much tenderness, so much warmth.

And if holding someone else's baby could make Isaac look this happy, she could only imagine his joy when he held a child of his own.

She sidled up to Isaac and put an arm around his waist. He turned to her with a bemused smile.

"She's so tiny," he murmured.

Cora couldn't resist giving him a kiss. Every time she thought she couldn't possibly love Isaac Muller any more, he surprised her.

"I promised Katie I'd bring her back," she told Isaac softly.

But Isaac didn't give Dorathea up right away. He smiled down into her face, and rocked her, and though he didn't make baby talk, it was plain he wanted to.

"Let me take her, Isaac."

Cora caressed his waist, hoping that he would feel in her touch what she could not say in front of Joes:

Yes, I promise you.

Isaac gingerly transferred the baby, but his eyes followed her wistfully as Cora took her in her arms, carried her away, and out of sight up the stairs.

When Cora returned, she wasn't surprised to notice that Isaac had fallen silent, and she made a point of entertaining Joes to cover up for it.

She glanced at Isaac now and then as she talked, and occasionally appealed to him for agreement, or some small comment, but his subdued expression went to her heart.

Soon Caleb came bounding in from outside, and threw himself into Joseph's lap, and then sat passively listening as they talked.

Isaac cast an almost pained look at his round, childish face and suddenly rose.

"I – I guess I have to get back, Joseph," he said apologetically. "I have errands for the shop this afternoon."

Joseph put out his hand. "We appreciate your help, Isaac. It was so kind of you and Cora to offer."

"We're happy for you and Katie," Isaac said. "Dorathea is a beautiful baby."

Joseph beamed at him. "Thank you."

Cora looked at him worriedly. "I'll come out with you, Isaac," she offered.

***

She followed Isaac outside, and they walked across the big lawn and out to the dirt road.

When they were alone, Cora reached out and took his hand.

Isaac shook his head, and looked away from her, out to the horizon.

“I know,” Cora murmured, trying to soothe him, but inside, she was wondering why she’d been so dense. She *hadn’t* known, or at least hadn’t guessed, just *how much* her husband wanted a baby.

And it made her feel guilty. If she was a good wife, she would’ve been more in tune with her husband.

Isaac wouldn’t pour out his feelings to her, that wasn’t his way. But he had already told her that he wanted children. He had set up a nursery in advance of a child.

Cora told herself that she should have seen this coming. But she was determined to correct it as soon as she could. Isaac’s disappointment melted her heart.

She pressed her lips on his hair. “We’ll have our own baby soon, Isaac,” she whispered.

He turned his head. “I know, Cora.” He leaned down and kissed her gently. “I’ll be back for you on Friday.”

Cora watched him climb into their buggy and drive away down the road. When it had disappeared, she walked back to the house, and was unusually quiet for hours after.

CHAPTER FIFTEEN

Early the next morning, Cora was one of the first ones up. She was about to start breakfast when a soft buzzing from inside her purse interrupted her. Cora looked around. The children were still upstairs, and Joes had disappeared outside.

Cora reached into her purse and pulled out the cell phone.

"Hello? Oh, hi Seth! You're up early!

"You're going to have to make it quick, I'm not at home.

"So -- you showed her the phone again? What did she say?

"I told you she would!" Cora laughed, and then clapped a hand over her mouth. She peered into the living room, but there was still no one else in sight.

"Oh, that's perfect. Yes, loan it to her, she won't tell. Did she say why she wanted it?"

Cora giggled again. "I *knew* she wanted that little blue

dress! Now, Seth, listen to me, when she gets it and wears it, you need to tell her how *sophisticated* she looks. Use a French word.

"I don't know, look one up. She loves art and French words and books – all that kind of thing, but don't *ever* tell her I told you, Seth! And don't lay the French words on too thick, or she'll guess!

"What? *Hmm.*

"You know, Seth, maybe it would help if she saw that *someone else knows you're cute.*

"Because you are, you know! You just have to work on your delivery.

"I have an idea. I want you to go to the youth sing next Sunday. Be sure to look your best. I'm going to send someone over, and I want you to flirt with her.

"I don't know yet. I'll work on it.

"You'll know when she flirts with you. Play along.

"You're welcome, Seth. Remember what I said about the phone.

"Bye."

Cora hung up and placed the phone back into its little hidden pocket. When she looked up, Joseph was standing in the front door, with his eyes on her.

"Cora, I gave you that phone for emergencies," he frowned, wiping his muddy shoes on the mat. "You shouldn't use it like a toy, and I don't want you using it *at all* in this house. I don't want the children to see it."

"But Joes, *you* have a phone," Cora objected, "and I'm just using mine to help a friend. Nobody knows."

"Does *Isaac* know?"

Cora looked down and shuffled her feet.

"No, of course not. Cora, I'm beginning to be sorry I gave you that thing. If you're wise, you'll use it seldom, or not at all."

"But it's *so* convenient, Joes," Cora said earnestly, "and so much fun! It has a little solar charger, and a calendar, and a clock, and you can see movies. Though the ones I've seen so far are gross."

"You shouldn't be watching movies *at all*. They're full of --"

"There's even a little game on this one. Look, Joes!"

She held up the screen, and a little delivery man jumped up in the air and over a wall.

Joseph's eyebrows formed a low, worried line over his eyes. "You're a grown woman, Cora," he said grimly, "and I can't tell you what to do. But if Isaac finds out, there will be trouble between you. And if anyone else finds out –"

"Oh, no one else will find out," Cora assured him.

"I pray that's true," Joseph sighed, and passed his hand over his eyes.

"Don't worry, Joes," Cora assured him brightly, "nothing bad will happen. I'm *very* careful."

Her brother looked at her grimly, and she could hear him muttering softly into his beard as he climbed the stairs.

Cora returned to preparing breakfast, and gave the dangers of phone use no more thought.

Her mind had already returned to Seth, and she was drawing up a mental list of helpers to send to the youth sing.

***

Cora's relationships had improved a lot after her wedding. Some of her childhood playmates had begun to be friendly again – she could only guess that they'd *finally* seen that she wasn't the shameless man-stealer that Leah Hauser had said.

Cora wiped the kitchen table down with a rag, considering possible accomplices. There was Becky King, who'd been seen *everywhere* with John Beiler until just a few days ago. The gossip was that they'd had a big fight. Maybe she'd be willing to flirt a little with Seth to show John that he wasn't the only boy in town.

May Lingerfelt was a very pretty girl, and Cora had been

close to her when they were young. Maybe she'd play along, if she was asked, just for fun.

Then there was Annie Hostetler, who was so boy crazy that she could be counted on to flirt with anyone. *Especially* if she had a little encouragement.

Cora put a finger to her lips.

Of course, she had to account for the probability that not all of them would said yes. Maybe *none* of them would say yes, so it made good sense to maximize her chances.

She would have to ask as many people as possible, in the hope that at least *one* of them would show up at the sing and make poor Seth look good to Mary.

And considering his awkwardness, she needed *all* the help she could get.

Cora cracked eggs and dropped them into a skillet. As she did, Emma came walking down the stairs.

She smiled apologetically at Cora. "I'm sorry to leave you alone with breakfast, Cora. I was hanging out the laundry. Is there something I can do to help you?"

Cora tilted her head.

"How old are you, Emma?"

"Fourteen. *Fifteen* next month," Emma replied.

Cora looked thoughtful. "That's only two years'

difference."

"What?"

Cora smiled at her winningly. "Would you be willing to do me a *favor*, Emma?"

"If I can."

"It would have to be our little secret."

Emma began to look wary. "What kind of favor?"

"Oh, nothing bad. It's just that I know a boy who's *head over heels* in love with a friend of mine. But she can't see how *cute* he is, and I want to help her see. I was thinking that if *another* girl showed him some attention, in front of her, she might see that he's a catch and be more friendly to him."

"What would you want *me* to do?" Emma stammered.

"Oh, nothing much. Just talk to him at the next Sunday sing. You know, smile at him, make big eyes, giggle. It would be fun -- he really is very cute."

"Who is it?"

Cora smiled her biggest, brightest smile. "It's Seth Troyer."

Emma goggled at her. "Seth *Troyer*? Do you want me to be a *laughing stock*?"

Cora put on a hurt expression. "Seth is *very* cute. Shy is the new sexy!"

"He's not *right*," Emma stammered, "he's like a – a – he reminds me of a bat!"

"He just hasn't had any practice with girls," Cora assured her. "Don't you think Seth deserves a chance at love, just like everybody else?"

"I *suppose*," Emma retorted, "but that's *his* lookout!"

"I'm surprised at you, Emma," Cora said, with a touch of reproach. "I would have thought you'd be more willing to help."

Emma's mouth fell open. "I – I –"

"Seth Troyer is a *very* handsome boy, I defy anyone to deny it. And there are worse ways to spend a Sunday evening than talking to a cute boy."

Emma's voice was almost pleading. "But – what if Seth thinks I *really* like him?"

"Don't worry, he knows it's all for show. I told you, he's in love with my friend."

"What friend?"

"Mary Stoltzfus."

Emma fell silent. At last she nodded.

"I hate to admit it, but – yes, I can see it. Mary is so

strange herself that no one but Seth would *ever* ask to court with her."

She looked up at Cora. "All right, Aunt Cora, I'll go and flirt with Seth. But only this *one* time. And only because it's a desperate case."

Cora hugged her ecstatically. "Oh, you're such a sweet girl, Emma," she soothed. "Stars in your crown!"

"I hope so," Emma retorted. "Because everyone else is going to think I'm crazy!"

CHAPTER SIXTEEN

Mary stood in front of the mirror, turning this way and that. The pretty navy blue dress fit her like a glove. It was classic and chic and made her look almost *French.*

Mary had worn jeans and tops before, but she'd never worn an English dress. After a lifetime in loose, modest Amish dresses, it felt too tight -- almost constricting.

But she *loved* the way it looked.

She slid her feet into the high-heeled pumps, and promptly fell over and almost turned her ankles.

How does anybody stand in these, she wondered, much less walk?

She put them on again and braced herself against the bed. The pumps might be painful to wear and hard to walk in, but they did magical things for her feet and legs. They looked so – *womanly*.

She took a baby step in the heels. Her foot wobbled, and she almost fell again, but she kept trying. She planned to attend the youth sing that evening wearing the dress *and* the heels.

It was her rumspringa, after all.

Mary met her own eyes in the mirror. She looked like a different person, and she was beginning to feel like one, too.

The English-looking girl smiled at her – and Mary smiled back.

***

When it was time to leave for the sing, Mary took off the heels and padded down the back stairs holding them in one hand. She didn't want her mother to catch sight of her in these English clothes, because she'd do several things, all of which Mary wanted to avoid: she'd be horrified by her clothes, and tell her to change immediately; she'd see it as a step toward total rebellion, and lecture her for weeks; and possibly – and this was what Mary feared the most – her mother would see it not as a statement of personal independence, but as a sign that Seth Troyer had somehow *gotten* to her, and that she was *primping* for him.

Mary set her mouth, thinking about it.

Because there would be plenty of *other* boys at the sing tonight, and she was curious just how many of *them* would notice her new look.

***

The sing that night was unusually well attended. Mary noticed half a dozen girls who weren't regulars, and some of them were also on rumspringa, and wearing English clothes.

Some of them waved, or came over and talked to her for a little while, which Mary had to admit, was a dramatic change in her social status.

She was also gratified to see some of the boys were casting surprised glances at her, though she pretended not to notice. But she had taken special care over her hair, and was wearing a little makeup, as well.

When the singing began, Mary felt well-satisfied with her experiment. It had already gone better than she had hoped. She felt comfortable in her new clothes, and she was cautiously optimistic that maybe, she might find the courage to dress like this more often.

And then --Seth Troyer arrived.

He crept in late, slid into one of the back benches, and immediately began to stare at her and *wave*.

Mary looked up at the ceiling, exquisitely conscious that *every eye in the room was on her*. The girls were trying to smother giggles, and some of the boys looked as if they felt sorry for her.

She looked down at her feet, trying to avoid making eye contact with Seth and fantasizing about what she was going to do to him if he ever, *ever* came within reach of her arm.

The singing seemed to last for a hundred years. When it finally dragged to a close, there was prayer, and then the formal part of the meeting broke up.

Mary glanced at the nearest door, wondering if she could escape before Seth reached her. She stood up and prepared to flee, but to her amazement, her way was blocked by a bevy of beautiful girls who – unbelievably – began calling out to *Seth*.

"*Hi*, Seth!"

"I've been wanting to talk to *you*, Seth."

"I was afraid you might not *show up* tonight, Seth!"

Mary watched in dumbfounded amazement as some of the most popular girls in the county mobbed Seth Troyer like an English rock star. Mary felt her mouth dropping open, and she wasn't the only one. Everybody else was staring like they couldn't believe their eyes.

May Lingerfelt had taken Seth's arm and was giggling like a preteen. Becky King squeezed up against him, Annie Hostetler was offering him chocolate and even shy little Emma Lapp was sitting at his feet as if she was dying of love.

Some of the boys snickered a little, no doubt thinking it was a joke, but when May Lingerfelt and Becky King began arguing over who was going to sit next to Seth for the rest of the evening, and Annie Hostetler took his hand in hers, they crossed their arms and frowned.

"Seth, are you going to be at the volleyball game next week?"

"Seth, will you come over and fix our porch swing? It's *broken*."

"Seth, I need someone to drive me to town."

"Oh, ladies," Seth was chuckling, "please! I can't think when I'm surrounded by such beautiful women."

Emma Lapp was the one wren among these birds of paradise, and Mary searched her face narrowly. But Emma's earnest expression was the very soul of purity.

Tears sparkled in her big eyes. "Seth, you said you were coming to the house yesterday," she reproached him. "And you *didn't*."

Mary sat down with a *thump*, feeling as if the whole room was in danger of flying away.

Seth looked up suddenly and seemed to notice her. "Well, *there you are*, Mary Stoltzfus!" he cried.

He shook off his admirers and crossed the room to sit down beside her. The girls followed him like puppies.

"So Mary, I was hoping to come over next week. I have a

book that I thought you'd like."

"*Settth*!" the girls whined, in unison.

"What about *me*, Seth?"

"You *promised*, Seth!"

"You got my *hopes* up, Seth."

Emma Lapp bit her lip and turned away.

Mary looked over Seth's shoulders and noticed that everyone in the room was staring at her, again. But this time, she didn't see amusement or pity. She could see that -- strange as it was – she was momentarily sharing in Seth's weird glory.

She rolled her eyes to his.

"Uh –"

"We'll call it settled, then," Seth declared, and his band of admirers sent up another wail.

CHAPTER SEVENTEEN

"You can say whatever you like, but *I know it was you.*"

It was lunchtime at the school, and Cora Muller sat serenely on a bench in the yard. Her expression was one of childlike innocence.

"I don't know what you're talking about, Mary Stoltzfus," she protested gently. "Why should you think that *I* had anything to do with it? Haven't I been telling you for months that Seth is gorgeous? It's clear that I'm not the *only* girl who noticed."

She paused and sighed. "He has the most *beautiful* green eyes! Almost as beautiful as Isaac's – but not quite."

"I saw your niece there too," Mary nodded grimly, "are you trying to tell me that *she* wasn't your accomplice?"

Cora giggled. "Emma has been *dying* for Seth for the last six months – poor little thing! He's *kind* to her, of course, but

– she's so young. She made up dream castles, I'm afraid."

Mary narrowed her eyes.

"Do you think I believe that the most popular girls in town are in love with that little weasel? What do you take me for?"

"Oh, Mary," Cora sighed patiently, "believe whatever you like. I don't understand what you have *against* Seth, but it doesn't matter. You saw for yourself how many other girls *adore* him. One of them will snap him up soon, and you won't have to worry about him anymore."

Mary fell silent, but stared at her friend's face in deep suspicion.

"He'll probably be *waiting* for me when I get home tonight," she scowled. "I have you to thank for this, Cora Muller!"

"I wish I could take credit for it, Mary," Cora said piously, and folded her hands. "You should *be* so lucky."

***

At the end of the day, Mary packed up her things and walked home from school. She briefly considered disappearing into the woods, and not coming out again until after dark. But then it occurred to her that if she wanted the truth, it would be much easier to pick Seth's brain, than Cora's.

The thought of grilling him gave her a certain grim satisfaction.

When she arrived at the house, she was relieved to see that Seth was nowhere in sight. She trudged up the porch steps and dumped her books on the dining room table. There was a sheaf of envelopes there.

She picked them up and riffled through them. There were a few for her.

"Is that you, Mary?" her mother called.

"Yes, mamm."

"Can you go out to the garden and bring in my basket? I think I left it there this morning."

"Okay."

Mary stuck the sheaf of envelopes in her pocket and walked out onto the porch. Sure enough, there was Seth Troyer walking up the path to the door, as if her irritation had conjured him up.

He smiled as he approached, and she had to admit, grudgingly, that he had white, even teeth.

"Hello, Mary."

She looked off into the distance. "Hello, Seth."

"I was hoping to catch you. I brought the book. I hope you like it."

He handed her a beautiful antique book of poetry. The book's cover was a dull red leather embossed with gold. It looked 19th century at least, and Mary reached for it in spite of herself.

She opened it and scanned its pages in wonder. It had beautiful calligraphy and illustrations.

And it was written entirely in *French.*

"Where did you *get* this, Seth?" she asked in wonder. "It's beautiful!"

"I bought it," he replied simply. "For you."

She looked up quickly and handed it back. "I can't take this!"

He shook his head. "You don't have to take it, Mary," he smiled. "Just borrow it. I want you to enjoy it. When you're finished reading it, you can give it back. But you can keep it as long as you like."

Mary stared at him in baffled embarrassment. "It's – it's really – generous of you, Seth," she stammered, "but you really didn't *need* to go to all –"

"I know," he shrugged. "I *wanted* to."

Mary bit her lip. Why did Seth Troyer *always* put her in an awkward position?

"Thank you, Seth. It's very nice of you." After such a

gesture, it was the only possible reply.

She looked at him grimly. She supposed that after he had given her a gift, it would be rude not to invite him in, or *something.*

She forced her lips to form the words: "Would you like to – stay to dinner, Seth?"

His face lit up. "Thank you, Mary! I'd love to! And if you don't mind my saying so," he added, "I thought the English dress you wore to the sing yesterday was *beautiful.*"

"Thank you, Seth," she said dully. "Do you mind waiting here for a minute while I fetch something? My mamm wanted her basket, and I need to get it before we go in."

"I'll be here."

Mary left him standing in the front yard, and walked around the side of the house to the garden. Her mother's basket was lying to one side of the patch. Mary picked it up, and the envelopes fell out onto the ground.

She sighed, and picked them up, and turned them over. None of them were interesting, except possibly one with no outward markings at all.

On an impulse, she tore the envelope open and unfolded the letter. It read:

Dear Ms. Stoltzfus:

It is our pleasure to inform you that you have been selected as one of six finalists in our essay contest. Congratulations!

Three of the six finalists will be selected as first, second and third prize winners.

In the next few weeks, the grand prize winner of an all-expense paid trip to Paris will be contacted. Second and third place winners will receive a thousand dollars each in the form of a check.

Congratulations on being selected as a finalist, and good luck!

Mary stared at the letter. She looked left, and looked right, and looked up at the sky.

Then she flailed her arms and screamed like a mad thing.

Soon Seth came tearing around the side of the house.

"Mary, what's wrong?" he yelped. "Why are you–?"

Before she could curb her excitement, Mary grabbed Seth by the ears, planted a frantic kiss right on his silly mouth, and bolted into the house. She would have done the same if Seth had been a horse.

But Seth Troyer stood trembling in the garden for a long while after, with his eyes staring and his mouth wide open.

CHAPTER EIGHTEEN

"I'm so glad you're back home. I've *missed* you."

Isaac Muller pulled his bride into his big arms. He bent down to meet her lips with a slow and communicative kiss.

"Mmm!" Cora mumbled, "Ah mes yu tew. Mm, oo tayse gud."

Isaac folded his arms around her and lifted her right up off the ground. Her feet kicked slowly in the air and her arms dangled over his back like a child's. Cora turned her face into his neck and giggled.

Isaac swatted her seat playfully. "Now come and make your husband some *dinner*. I'm starving!"

"Kiss me, Isaac."

"I'm too weak. I've had nothing but canned food for three days."

"Oh, *poor* Isaac," she whispered, nibbling his ear.

"There's nothing in the pantry but potted meat and last year's cabbage!"

"*Kiss* me."

"Make me some *dinner*, Cora," he begged. "Something *hot*! Make me some sausage and biscuits. Or some ham and peas!"

"Not until you *kiss* me."

He shook his head and whispered into her ear: "That's what you *always* say, and it *always* means that I starve until midnight. I'm going on strike until you cook me some food."

"Oh, all right." Cora giggled, "If you're going to be *that way* about it." She wriggled out of Isaac's arms and led him into the kitchen.

Isaac sat down at the kitchen table as Cora busied herself with the pots and pans.

"Katie sends her love," she told him, as she rummaged in the little refrigerator. "She said to tell you that she appreciates our help. She looks so much stronger already, I think she'll be back up in a few more days. She's already starting to complain about having to stay in bed," she laughed.

"Oh, and that reminds me, Isaac," she added sweetly, "that basket I brought home is a gift to you from Katie. She said she felt sorry for you, having to fend for yourself *all alone*."

Isaac's blue eyes brightened.

"What's in it?"

"It's a smoked ham and a –"

Cora turned and her words trailed out into the air. Isaac had disappeared.

***

When he came back in, they ate dinner, and talked for a long time, and then went downstairs to the moonlit lawn and lay down under the big oak tree. Isaac welcomed her home in the mottled silver shade until the moon was high in the sky. Cora looked up, and the stars winked down at her through the new leaves, as if they were happy, too.

Only the chill of deep night cooled their kisses, and they parted slowly and reluctantly.

After they had gone up to bed, Cora lay in bed looking out through the big picture window. It was well after midnight. The window was thrown open and a cool, delicious breeze made the curtain flutter. A solitary star shone in the night sky.

Isaac was fast asleep.

Cora reached out and played idly with his silky hair. The white tendrils curled around her hand like a baby's fingers.

Maybe *this* would be the night.

Oh Lord, Cora prayed, he wants children so badly. Please help us get pregnant. I want to give him a baby.

Lord, it's true I don't really want a child as badly as Isaac does, but I don't mind starting early if that's what he wants.

I promise to try hard to be a good parent. I'm not as wise as Katie, or as good, but I really will do my best.

She stroked Isaac's curls lightly, watching him as he slept. The faint moonlight from the window just touched his lashes, the curve of his cheek, the pillow of his lips. His face was as peaceful as a child's.

He was beautiful.

Cora's fingers barely grazed his cheek, his jaw. Isaac's babies would be beautiful, too, with round blue eyes and white hair and chubby little cheeks. They would be sturdy and healthy and heavy in her arms.

They would be sunny, happy babies that would only cry if they were *hungry*.

She smiled and tapped his lower lip with her finger.

Isaac had spent dinner telling her about what had happened while she was gone. Hans Miller had finally given him his performance review, and it had gone very well. He had told her, with a shy smile, that Mr. Miller had given him a raise and the promise of more work than he could do. Isaac had tried to be low-key about it, but she could tell that he was pleased.

He had shrugged and told her – trying to sound nonchalant – that his boss had told him that he was a *true craftsman*. That he had a *gift*.

That wasn't news to *her*, but Isaac had actually gone red when he told her.

He wasn't at all vain, and he didn't seek praise. Cora knew that he was happy because he was thinking of her, of their financial security.

And of those future babies that he clearly wanted so much.

She leaned over and kissed his cheek as lightly as a sigh, but Isaac's lids fluttered open. He raised his arm behind his head sleepily.

"I'm sorry. I didn't mean to wake you," she whispered.

"You're still up?"

"I was watching you sleep," she smiled. "You look so sweet when you're sleeping, Isaac."

"Hmm." He put his arm around her shoulder, and she pillowed on his chest.

"What were you dreaming about?"

He didn't answer.

"You looked like you were dreaming about something

good."

He squeezed her arm, but was silent.

She kissed his chin. "You're *supposed* to say that you were dreaming about *me*."

"I do dream about you, Cora," he murmured.

"But not tonight?"

"Not in the same way as usual."

"What then?"

"I just dreamed about what we did today. About riding with you in the buggy, and kissing you in the living room. About having dinner with you, and – and about how good and *right* it feels when I make love to you. I just dream about our life."

Cora received this in silence. He said nothing more, and sleep slowly took them both as she lay there on his chest.

CHAPTER NINETEEN

The next day was Saturday, but Cora was still up fairly early. At dawn she was in her kitchen, cleaning up after breakfast.

The kitchen windows faced out on the back yard, and the side street flanking the house. Cora loved them, but the openness still made her feel oddly exposed.

It was awkward, being so close in town. Unless they pulled the shades down, the interior of their home was a fish bowl for passers-by to see into. Even at that quiet hour it felt strange to Cora. She was used to living in the country, with the nearest neighbors miles away.

So far, it hadn't been a problem, though. They were on the farthest edge of town, on a mostly deserted commercial street. There was an empty storefront on one side of the house, and a small house for rent on the other. The only curious eyes that morning had belonged to a stray cat padding down the narrow side street.

Cora was glad that her kitchen windows faced down onto an empty street, because it was clear that she was going to be in the kitchen often. She was learning that her six-foot-plus husband required a *lot* of maintenance when it came to food.

She looked down at the sink and sighed: this morning's extravaganza had required two skillets, three platters, five plates, four small bowls for condiments and gravies, four serving spoons, two pitchers, a coffee pot, four glasses, and two cups. It had taken her thirty minutes to clean it all up.

Isaac was already out in the back yard, gathering tools. He had planned to use his off day to work on their kitchen garden. He was going to prepare a little plot for her tomatoes and peppers and beans.

Cora peeked out at him. He was hard at work already, digging out a neat square for planting. It was probably safe to assume that he was going to be busy for a long time.

Cora wiped her hands on her apron and fetched her bag from behind the couch.

She tapped in a number and cast a quick glance back at the kitchen windows.

"Hi, Seth. Is it too early?

"Good. I just wanted to find out how it went."

She listened for a few minutes, and an incredulous smile dawned over her face. "No – *all* of them?" She threw her head back and laughed delightedly.

“Oh, Seth, I never thought they’d *all* come! What did she do?

Cora nodded. “I *knew* she would. How did she look?

“Oh, you’re just a romantic, Seth. --You did what? Oh, that was *so* sweet!

“I’ll bet she took it, too. Didn’t she?

“What? Kissed you?

“On the mouth?

“No, I didn’t have anything to do with *that*!

“What paper?

Cora lapsed into amazed silence. “I don’t know.” She began to giggle. “Does it *matter*?

“I could try to find out for you. But the important thing is that you’re *in* now.

“I think so. You just need to keep being sweet and saying the right things. Mary is hard to get to know, but once she likes you, she *likes* you.

“No, she won’t show you. At least, not right away.

“But I *never* thought –”

The sound of Isaac’s footsteps on the stairs made Cora turn

her head. “Seth, I have to go!” she blurted, and threw the phone back into her bag. She dumped it on the kitchen table and sat down hurriedly.

There had been no time for any more. Isaac was already walking in.

He plopped down at the kitchen table beside her and scattered a handful of spades and pots in front of his wife.

“Whew!” he sighed. “All done! But I have to go to the store for the plants. You have a few dollars in your bag, don’t you Cora?”

He reached for her purse, and opened it.

Cora watched him with her mouth open. She hadn’t had time to hide her cell phone.

Isaac looked down into her bag, frowned, and pulled something out. Cora sent up a silent prayer for mercy, but it was too late.

Isaac’s blue eyes held dismay.

“What’s this?”

Cora’s cheeks went beet red. Her cell phone was lying there in Isaac’s big palm like a stolen thing. She was *busted* -- and there was no way out.

Joe’s dire words of warning came back to her, but it was too late now.

"I –"

"Cora, you know that the *Ordnung* forbids this. You swore to obey! I'm *surprised* at you – and so soon after your vow!"

"Isaac, it's just –"

Isaac raised troubled eyes on her face. "Did you buy this yourself?"

Cora looked down and shook her head.

"Who bought this for you?"

Cora looked at him unhappily. "If I tell you, Isaac, will you keep it a secret?"

He nodded. "*Who was it?*"

"It was Joes," Cora admitted, "But he only did it in case I had an emergency, like he had with Katie. That's all that he was thinking of, Isaac."

"But we live in the middle of *town*, Cora," Isaac reminded her quietly. "There are people all around us! And you were talking to one of your friends just now. I heard you!"

Cora looked up at him pleadingly, but his expression was unyielding.

She squirmed uncomfortably. "*Yes*."

"And it was just lying loose in your bag, where anybody might see it!" he marveled. "If you were caught, you might even have been *shunned* for this," he said, looking down at the phone as if it was a snake. "And then I – your husband! – I'd have to –"

"Oh, Isaac, if I was caught, I'd repent *right away*," Cora assured him earnestly.

He stared at her incredulously. Finally he replied:

"Cora, I -- I'm going to *destroy* this thing, and I want you to *promise* me that you will never put your hand on a cell phone again. Or anything else that the *Ordnung* forbids us."

Cora wilted under the stern expression on his face.

"I'm sorry, Isaac. I *promise*."

He nodded, and took the cell phone in his hands. He lifted his pinky fingers ceremoniously, gave his wrists a twist, and the cell phone snapped like a saltine. A little shower of small plastic shards rained down on the table.

Cora felt her lips turning down into a pout. It was Isaac's disapproval, far more than the loss of the phone, that hurt.

That, and knowing that she had disappointed him.

"Now, I'm going out into the back yard, and I'm going to *bury* it," Isaac told her solemnly. "And we won't speak of it, *ever again*."

Cora nodded, and looked down at her hands. As he walked out, she grumbled a little under her breath, only to hear his voice from the next room:

"I *heard* that, Cora."

Cora tossed her head a little, and subsided into wounded silence.

CHAPTER TWENTY

Later that afternoon, Joseph looked up from his front yard to see Isaac Muller's buggy approaching. He wiped his brow with one arm and stopped work on the little wooden play pen he had been building.

The buggy came to a stop at the mailbox, and Isaac got out. One look at his face made Joseph pull his mouth down in a rueful grimace.

Isaac had found Cora's phone.

"Good afternoon, Isaac!"

For once in his life, Isaac's face was not placid. He stared steadily into his brother-in-law's eyes.

"I need to talk to you *privately*, Joseph Lapp."

Joseph sighed and nodded. "You can talk to me here. The children are at their grandparent's."

Isaac looked down at his feet, as if he was gathering his speech.

"I found out today that Cora has been using a *cell phone*. She says that you gave it to her."

Joseph bit his lip and nodded. "That's right."

Isaac's eyes snapped up. "Cora is my *wife* now, Joseph Lapp. You have no right to give her such a thing without my knowledge."

Joseph nodded again. "I gave her the phone before the two of you were married, Isaac," he replied. "For emergencies. I warned her to use it sparingly, and only when she really needed to. But… she… *seldom* pays attention to what I tell her."

"*How* could you give her such a thing at all, knowing what could've happened-" Isaac bit off the rest of his words and looked down again.

Joseph sighed and put his arm around Isaac's shoulder. "Come and sit down, Isaac," he said, and after a momentary hesitation, Isaac allowed himself to be led up to the front porch. The two men sat down in the wicker chairs.

"I understand why you're angry, Isaac," he said quietly. "If Cora had been found out, it might have been terrible. But I was thinking of her safety. She almost died once because she had no good way to reach out for help. I didn't want that to *ever* happen again."

Isaac stared at the ground and said nothing.

"I have a cell phone, *too,* Isaac. I bought it when Katie was having her trouble, because I was worried. What if she needed help right away? What if the minutes counted? I'm a new father again. I think about these things more and more. I would rather see my family in trouble, than to see them hurt."

Isaac frowned. "What about the Ordnung, Joseph. What about her vow?"

Joseph looked up at the ceiling. "Yes, I know she vowed. But maybe the Ordnung should be changed."

"Maybe it should. But not like this. And not with *Cora*."

Joseph's eye glinted. "I wasn't using Cora to change the Ordnung, Isaac."

Isaac passed a hand over his eyes and shook his head. "No, Joseph. No, you didn't mean to use Cora. But if this question ever comes up before the elders, it shouldn't be *because of Cora*. If I hadn't found her phone today, that's how it might've happened! She was in danger once, yes, out among the English. But she's back at home now, and there's no such danger here. She's my wife now, Joseph Lapp -- it's *my* job to protect her. Part of that job is to keep her from being *shunned*, and driven out to the English *again*!"

Joseph was struck silent, and seeing that he had nothing to say, Isaac added: "Cora has promised me that she will not take a cell phone into her hand, ever again. I want you to promise me, Joseph Lapp, that you will never again *tempt* her with one."

Joseph nodded. "All right, Isaac. I promise."

He trained his bright eyes on Isaac's face. "But remember, I know Cora even better than you do. She means well, but she's never been good with rules. Are you going to make her promise not to try every little thing she sees and wants? There are going to be a lot of them! If you want to keep Cora out of trouble, Isaac, you're going to have to convince her that it's safe for her to talk to you about what she's doing, even if you don't like it. Otherwise, she'll hide her mischief, and you'll be surprised like this over and over again."

Isaac stood up abruptly. "I've said what I came to say," he announced, and paused at the edge of the porch steps before delivering this parting shot:

"I'm *very* upset with you, Joseph Lapp!"

Joseph's eyebrows twitched up in bemusement. He watched Isaac stalk off to the buggy, climb in, turn the horse, and ride away.

After a few minutes, a faint noise from behind the screen door made him turn his head.

"All right, go ahead and say it," Joseph sighed.

Katie appeared with the sleeping baby in her arms. She leaned against the door frame and shook her head.

"It's not my place to scold you, Joseph," she replied piously.

He raised his eyebrows and twisted around to look at her. "Since when? Come."

He put out his arms, and Katie came and sat down in the chair beside him.

"I'm afraid I've really offended him," he murmured. "I've never seen him so upset before."

"Oh, he'll calm down," Kate assured him. "Give him some time to think about what you said. Isaac has always been reasonable."

Joseph shook his head. "When was he ever *reasonable* about Cora? Remember what he did to that little monster that attacked her? I was the first one there that night, and I've never seen anything like it. I thought the boy was dead!"

"Of *course* Isaac is protective of Cora," she replied. "He has a strong instinct that way, and it's flaring up now. But you gave Cora the phone before they were married. It was *Cora's* responsibility to tell him about it, not yours. Isaac is an honest man, and sooner or later, he'll admit that. "Maybe, someday, even to *you*."

Joseph reached out and caressed the sleeping baby. "Oh, I don't need confirmation, Kate," he sighed. "I've watched Cora all my life. God *help* Isaac, because he's going to need all the help he can *get*."

CHAPTER TWENTY-ONE

Cora ran to the door when Isaac returned to their apartment. He was standing on the little landing outside their apartment, looking grim and tired.

"Oh, Isaac, I hope you weren't *mean* to Joes," she fretted.

Isaac took off his hat wearily and entered. "I was not *mean* to your brother," he replied. "Sit down, Cora, I want to talk to you."

Cora sat down beside him on the sofa and looked up at him with guilty expectancy.

Isaac returned her gaze solemnly. "Cora, I told Joseph that I didn't like that he gave you a cell phone without telling me."

"But, *Isaac* –"

He put up his hand, and she fell silent.

"That was bad. But what was *worse*, Cora, was that *you*

didn't tell me."

Cora's mouth drooped like a scolded child's. She looked away from him.

"You've hidden this from me for *months*. It wasn't a small secret, Cora! If you'd been caught, it could've wrecked our *lives*."

Tears sprang out in Cora's eyes. "I didn't mean any harm, Isaac," she said, in a small, wounded voice.

"Why didn't you tell me, Cora?"

Cora bit her lip. "It was just – I didn't want to upset you."

"But you didn't think I'd be upset when I found out that you hadn't told me the truth?"

"I didn't *lie* to you, Isaac," Cora pointed out earnestly. "I just didn't – *share*."

Isaac's expression was troubled, but patient. "But we're married now, Cora. We're *supposed* to share. It's unhealthy to hold back. Why did you even use a cell phone at all? There was no need!"

Cora avoided his gaze. "I did it – it did it because *Mary Stoltzfus needs a man*, Isaac."

Isaac stared at her.

"What?"

Cora looked up at him with big, pleading eyes. "Mary is *such* a sweet girl, Isaac, but she won't get her nose out of a book long enough to even *look* at any boys, and poor little Seth Troyer is just *dying* of love for her, and I thought, if I could only get Mary to *notice* Seth, then he might have a chance. And since Mary doesn't have a cell phone –"

Isaac closed his eyes and raised his brows. "Cora, what are you *talking* about? You risked our future, you risked getting *shunned*, so that your friend could get a *date*?"

"You make it sound so *bad*, Isaac! And it wasn't, really! No one ever saw the phone except you, and Seth."

Isaac opened his eyes again. "Seth Troyer knows you had a phone."

"Yes, he was the one I always talked to," Cora explained. "But don't worry, Isaac, Seth will never tell! But even if someone else *had* seen it, even if I'd gotten into trouble, I would've just repented -- and then everything would have been all right!"

Isaac sat in silence for a long moment. "Cora," he said finally, "if this had gotten out, things would *not* have been all right. It scares me to think how close we came to *big trouble*."

He gave her a direct look. "It's all because you kept this thing a secret from me. And that *hurts*, Cora. It *hurts* to think that you didn't *trust* me enough to tell me."

Cora’s mouth formed a horrified O. Tears began to roll down her cheeks.

“Oh, Isaac, I never meant to hurt you!” she cried, and cast herself onto his chest. “No, no, it wasn’t that I didn’t trust you, not that at all! I trust you more than anyone else in the *world*!”

Isaac’s bravado crumbled under Cora’s kisses. His arms went around her, and he buried his face in her bright hair.

But he gave it one last try.

“Cora, you have to *promise* me –”

“Yes, yes,” she was sobbing, “I promise anything, Isaac! The very idea, that I would *ever* hurt you! Oh, my darling!”

Isaac gave up, and the last shreds of his resolve were swept away before a torrent of tear-stained love.

***

But later that evening, when they were lying in bed, Cora felt his eyes on her in the darkness.

“What?” she asked softly.

He didn’t answer, and looked down at the coverlet.

“*What*, Isaac? You’ve been staring at me all night. Are you still angry?”

He shook his head.

"*Don't* be angry, Isaac," she pleaded.

He shook his head. "That's just it, Cora. I've never been *really* mad at you, never once. And I think sometimes I *need* to be."

"Why?"

"Because you're reckless, Cora. You're going to get in trouble. You don't take things seriously enough."

Cora got quiet. After a long time she answered: "That depends on what you mean, Isaac. I take some things *very* seriously. Like seeing my friend ruin her life by turning away a sweet, handsome boy who adores her and just wants to be *loved*. I'm not saying the *Ordnung* isn't important, Isaac. It *is*. But isn't *loving* and *being loved* more important than all this fuss about a silly cell phone?"

Isaac reached out and caressed her cheek. "Yeah. I guess it is, Cora. But the elders wouldn't see it that way, if they found out you'd been using one."

He leaned over and kissed her gently.

"Now go to sleep. We're going to need our rest," he sighed. "Tomorrow is Sunday worship, and after all you've been up to, we'd both better go and pray. Hard."

CHAPTER TWENTY-TWO

Mary Stoltzfus lay draped across her bed, reading by the yellow light of a kerosene lamp.

Her bedside clock read 1 a.m., and she was going to have to get up in a few hours to get ready for worship, but she couldn't bring herself to put down the beautiful antique book that Seth Troyer had given her.

Her secret study of French had paid off: to her surprise, she could read and understand most of the poems.

They were *beautiful.*

The words transported Mary straight to a medieval chateau filled with knights and noble ladies. She mouthed the words rapturously.

Petals floating on the wind

Remind me of your kiss, my faithless love

So soft, and so soon gone, my lady fair.

Mary pressed the book to her breast, and closed her eyes. She saw a forlorn knight, idly twirling a flower between his fingers. She opened the book again.

The night birds call, sweetly, sweetly

One to another, one to another

But you will not answer me.

I wait in vain!

She sighed and imagined a lonely swain, lingering outside his lady love's dark window. His expression was one of longing and *wounded love.*

How could you turn from me so soon,

Belladonna, queen of mysteries?

Who will live in your heart tonight,

O you who have stolen mine?

Mary closed her eyes rapturously and clasped the book to her heart. It was *so romantic.* She could *see* the rejected lover, searching for his lady love with restless, unhappy eyes.

There was, however, one significant drawback to these pleasant dreams. Occasionally Mary's thrilling fantasies were defiled by the mental image of Seth Troyer's face.

But that didn't trouble Mary half as much as the fact that

somehow, her memory of Seth's face had *changed.* Previously, she had seen only Seth's laughable worminess.

Now – and it *bothered* her – she was, occasionally, seeing his *green eyes*. Or his *white teeth.*

Mary looked down at the book. She had to wonder if Seth knew what these poems were about, and if so, she wondered if he'd chosen them deliberately to make her see him as a wounded lover, pining for his lady. It would be just like him.

But she was sure of one thing: Cora Muller had clearly had nothing to do with *this*. Cora had no interest in poetry of any kind, and certainly not historical poetry.

This was Seth *all the way*.

Mary flipped through the pages of the book. It was an antique, a real work of art, with calligraphy and antique pen illustrations on every page. It clearly had been an expensive purchase, and she wondered how much it had cost Seth.

She couldn't keep it, of course: she was going to have to give the book back, and she planned to urge Seth to return it.

But she had to admit that it was an exquisite object, and that the gift was a beautiful gesture. It seemed that in spite of his awkward exterior, Seth Troyer was a real romantic.

Mary closed the book reluctantly and put it aside.

It was really kind of a shame that he was such a *worm*.

Mary leaned over and blew out the lamp, and the room went dark. She tried to banish her thoughts, and to settle down for sleep.

But to her dismay, Cora's words came back in her memory: "You saw for yourself how many other girls *adore* him. One of them will snap him up soon, and you won't have to worry about him anymore."

Mary turned over restlessly, and crammed her pillow over her ears. Cora Muller was a busybody and she absolutely could *not* be trusted when it came to Seth and Mary was 99 percent sure that Cora had orchestrated that mob scene at the sing and that it was totally fake and that Seth Troyer was a *worm*.

But in spite of this certainty, Seth Troyer's laughing face, and the adoring smiles of his female admirers, haunted Mary's dreams all that night.

***

The next morning came far too early for Mary. The sound of her mother rapping on the bedroom door sifted down to her through a thick layer of sleep. The cloud lifted just enough for Mary to roll out of bed, eat, and get dressed. She was half asleep when she climbed into the family buggy after breakfast, and she actually dozed a little on the way to worship.

It was a bright, beautiful day in late spring. The

community had gathered at Amon Lapp's huge farm, and the buggies covered the countryside.

Mary climbed out of her parent's buggy, shading her sleepy eyes. The sun was almost too bright for her.

She hung back behind her parents as they walked to the seating area set up on the lawn. Since it was worship, Mary's parents had insisted she wear her prim blue Sunday dress. Mary had to admit that the dress was certainly achieving its function: it made her feel *plain.*

Mary felt a twinge of guilt. She had been enjoying her rumspringa by buying and wearing all kinds of English clothes; but the result was that now, she was no longer happy in her usual clothes. She was sure that the bishop would've had something to say about that feeling, if he knew of it.

But that was the least of her worries. As she sat down beside her mother on the women's benches, and the long, slow worship songs began, Mary's mind wandered to the letter she had received.

What would she do if, by some miracle, she actually *won the trip to Paris*?

Her mother knew that she'd entered a contest, but it would be hard to justify to anyone else. She was competing against others in an attempt to prove that she was the better writer. The first prize was a vacation to Paris.

If she won, it would be seen, *literally,* as her *ego trip*.

Plus, if she won the trip to Paris, she'd have to fly. Airplane travel was discouraged, except in emergencies.

She would be going to a foreign country, by herself. Her trip to New York had made her less afraid of travel, but at least *Cora* had been with her then. This time, she'd be completely *alone*.

Mary closed her eyes.

Her parents would never allow it. Her father, in particular, would reject it out of hand. He might be willing to overlook some English clothing, but a trip to a foreign country, alone? It simply wasn't going to happen.

That is, if she *told* them about it.

The singing wound to a close, and there was prayer. Mary bowed her head, and her guilt returned.

If she won the contest, the only way she could ever hope to get permission would be to invent some plausible story that would explain a week-long absence. There were precious few possibilities.

And, no matter what she came up with, it would be a *lie*.

Mary's eyebrows twitched together.

There was one other way, a way that didn't involve lying, but Mary frankly doubted she'd have the courage to do it.

She could tell her parents boldly that she had won the

contest, that she was going to Paris, and that she didn't care what anybody thought of it.

And then, accept the consequences.

The prayer ended, and they all sat down. One of the preachers stood up and began the sermon.

Mary chewed her nail. What would happen to her if she won the contest, and then -- simply told the truth?

Probably nothing good. Of course, no one could stop her from going to Paris, but what would she face when she returned? She'd never heard of anyone else doing such a thing.

Of course, she was still on her rumspringa, and that was in her favor, but she had no way of knowing what would happen.

She'd been thrilled when she'd received the letter, but now Mary was glad that she'd kept it a secret. At least she had time to think privately about what she'd do if she won.

Mary looked at her mother out of the corner of her eye.

But she had to admit, now that she'd gamed it out, she was almost hoping that she *wouldn't*.

CHAPTER TWENTY-THREE

After worship, there was lunch inside the house, and Mary endured it in silence. She wasn't in the mood for fellowship.

After the meal, she excused herself, and walked out of the house, looking for a secluded place to think until it was time to go.

There was a big oak tree to one side of the house, conveniently screened by a line of bushes, and Mary made for it. There was no one else around, and she plopped down beside the ancient trunk, and leaned against it.

Mary looked up at the sky through the new leaves. She felt guilty. She shouldn't be thinking about English clothes, she shouldn't be trying to prove she was better than others, and she shouldn't be dreaming about going to a city that was world famous for its vices.

Even if it was *also* world famous for its art and learning.

Maybe she *was* taking her rumspringa too far. The Amish faith had thrived for hundreds of years because of its firm boundaries. For most Amish people, they worked very well.

A new and terrible thought clutched at Mary's throat.

What if she wasn't one of them?

What if she went to Paris – and liked it better than home?

***

"Can I join you?"

Mary lowered her eyes. It was, of course, Seth Troyer.

For some reason he looked *marginally* less geeky than she remembered. Maybe it was his hair. He did have very shiny brown hair, and the mottled sunlight painted it with gold highlights.

She stifled a sigh. "Okay."

He sat down beside her and smiled. "Did you read the book?"

Mary shrugged. "I took a look at it."

She was suddenly very relieved that Seth didn't know what the book was actually about – but to her embarrassment, her relief was premature.

"I thought it was beautiful expression of chivalric love," he said earnestly, training his eyes on hers. "Didn't *you*?"

In her amazement, Mary forgot to be irritated. "You read *French*?"

Seth shook his head. "No. But I used a translation feature on the internet to read what it said."

Mary stared at him, and a spark of her old irritation returned. "We're really not supposed to do things like that, Seth," she reminded him. "Aren't you worried that you're going to get in trouble?"

"I might, it's true," he agreed. "But I'm on my rumspringa, and isn't that what it's supposed to be for? To try English things, to see what else is out there? At least, that's what I think."

"I do, *too*," Mary mumbled. "But how far is *too* far? That's what I'd like to know."

"I guess you don't know until you go there," Seth replied. He raised his green eyes to hers. "But when it comes to *you*, Mary, I don't care about the risk."

Mary looked off to the horizon. "I wish you'd stop saying things like that, Seth. It puts me in an awkward position."

Seth looked down and pulled a blade of grass out of the ground.

"I know that you're not looking for a man in your life right now, Mary," he shrugged. "But to be honest, that's one of the things I *like* about you. It's plain to me that you have big plans for yourself – maybe even a career. So do *I*."

Mary turned and looked at him. "What do you mean?"

Seth continued to pull blades of grass. "I mean that I might not decide to join the church. I might apply to an English school and get a degree."

Mary's mouth fell open. She had never heard anyone say such a thing before.

"So – what do you want to be, Seth?" she asked, and to her own surprise, she was interested in the answer.

"I like designing things. I think I might be a good engineer, if I could get the education."

Mary shook her head. "But how would you ever get the *money*, Seth?"

"I've thought about it. I might be able to get a scholarship and work my way through school."

"But what about your family? They'd be crushed that you didn't join the church."

He nodded. "I was thinking of becoming a Mennonite, but of course, my folks want me to be Amish. That's why I haven't said anything about it to anyone."

Mary stared at him. "Except… *me*."

Seth shrugged, and continued to pull blades of grass.

Mary pinched her lips into a straight line and looked off into the distance. She could acquit Seth of making up a story to play on her sympathies. He wasn't crafty.

But he had a positive *genius* for putting her in awkward, embarrassing, *impossible* positions.

"Look, Seth, maybe you should keep all that to yourself, at least until you're ready to do it," she replied in exasperation. "You could get people upset. I won't rat you out, but *really* -- it's not the sort of thing you should blab about!"

He looked up at her, and his voice was earnest and warm. "Oh, I know *you* won't say anything, Mary."

Mary stared at him grimly. "And *about* that book –"

He looked down at the ground again. "I was hoping you'd have the chance to read it, Mary. It kind of – said all the things I wanted to say, and didn't have the words."

Mary gaped at him, and suffered a full-body surge of mortification.

"Seth, that's – that's –"

"Oh, I know you're not thinking about that right now. But I couldn't help it, you know?"

Mary's shoulders drooped in defeat. What could she possibly say to *that*?

"I may never have the nerve to ask this again, Mary. But

can I – can I *kiss* you?"

Mary sighed. She was thinking: If it will make you go away, Seth.

She nodded mutely and closed her eyes.

Seth leaned forward, and gave her a shy, soft peck on the lips.

When she opened her eyes, he was beaming.

"Oh, Mary, it was *just* like I dreamed it," he was saying – and she stifled the impulse to turn and beat her head against the tree trunk.

CHAPTER TWENTY-FOUR

Cora's brows twitched together. She shook biscuit flour off of her hands and peered out the window of the little apartment.

It was only a little past lunchtime, and the straw hat bobbing just under the window told her that Isaac was back from work.

Four hours *too early*.

She wiped her hands on a dish towel and went to open the door.

When it swung open, Isaac was just standing outside, looking at the ground. As soon as he raised his eyes, Cora knew that something bad had happened – something *very* bad.

"What's wrong, Isaac?" She put a hand on his arm and pulled him inside.

He walked in and sat down heavily on the couch. He didn't say anything for a while.

Finally he replied: "Hans Miller had a heart attack at the shop today, Cora."

"*Ach nein*!" Cora gasped, and put a hand to her mouth.

"He passed away an hour ago."

"Oh, Isaac!" Cora reached out for him. "Oh, Isaac, how *awful*! How *awful* for his family!"

Isaac looked down at his hands.

"He was a good man. A fair employer." He shook his head. "The family closed the shop for the day. But some of us have decided to go in tomorrow, just to help them keep their orders while they make the arrangements."

"What happened, Isaac? Was he upset about something, or, or *sick*?"

Isaac shook his head. "Not that I ever saw. He was always smiling, and he never missed a day of work."

Cora reached out and caressed his face. "I'll make a casserole. We can take it over to his family tomorrow."

Isaac nodded. "I still can't believe it," he marveled. "He looked fine this morning. He went into his office to make some phone calls, and he just – collapsed. Gideon found him."

"It's *terrible.* How old was he?"

"Forty-three."

"*Ohh*," Cora groaned.

Isaac took her in his arms, and said nothing more: but his round blue eyes stared at the wall beyond her shoulder as if he was seeing something else.

***

Hans Miller's funeral was held three days later at his home. Cora and Isaac attended, along with a good portion of the county: Mr. Miller had been a well-known businessman.

Cora stood miserably in the Miller's living room, saying little, and listening to the sound of hushed voices and quiet sniffing. She hated funerals, and for the moment she was alone: Isaac had gone off to express his condolences to Hans Miller's widow.

Han Miller's son, Gideon, was standing in the doorway talking quietly to the bishop. Gideon was the eldest son, as quiet and solemn as his father had been warm and outgoing. Cora felt sorry for him, but she hadn't gone to greet him: she wasn't sure that the gesture would be appreciated. Gideon Miller wasn't very approachable at the best of times, and now he looked patently miserable.

Isaac came back into the room, walked up to Gideon, and put his hand on his shoulder. Cora noticed that her instinct had been correct. Gideon did not look comforted by Isaac's kindness: if anything, he looked *more* distressed. He said a few short words and looked away.

Cora felt her face going warm at Gideon's rudeness, but told herself that anger would be unfair. It was his father's funeral. Gideon was not himself.

But even so, it gave her an uneasy feeling. Gideon would be Isaac's new employer at the shop. And since Isaac had rented their apartment from Hans Miller, he was also their new landlord.

Looking at his distant, uncomfortable expression, Cora couldn't help feeling just a little worried.

The funeral service was long and somber, and when it was over, Isaac and Cora drove their buggy out to the burial site with dozens of other mourners. It was overcast and unseasonably chilly, and though she felt guilty for it, Cora was heartily glad when the service was over and they could go back home. They left the buggy at a rented stable on the edge of town, and walked the remaining block to the little house.

The wind had picked up, and when they arrived home, it was whistling around the corners of the little house. The branches of the oak tree tossed in the air, and here and there new leaves floated past the windows and blew down the street.

Cora busied herself in the kitchen, lighting the stove and opening the refrigerator. There had been plenty of food at the Miller's, but Isaac had been silent all the way home, and in Cora's expert opinion, her husband needed a pie and coffee at *least*, and probably some ice cream after.

As she broke out the pecans and sugar, Cora admitted to herself that after the day they'd had, *she* wouldn't mind a little comfort food, either.

She baked sawdust pie, Isaac's favorite, and filled the little house with warmth and the smell of roasting pecans. To Cora's relief, the scent drew Isaac into the kitchen, and inspired him to open the oven door and scoop some of the pie filling right from the pan.

He blew it cool, and took a bite. "*Mmm*, Cora. You sure know how to take the edge off a hard day," he sighed.

She poured out a steaming cup of coffee, and served up a hot piece of pie topped with a generous dollop of ice cream. Isaac ate them with an expression of slow relish.

She let him finish, kissed the taste of pecans and coconut off his lips, and then climbed into his lap like a child. She twined her arms around his neck and rested her head on his shoulder.

Isaac folded her in his arms and kissed her hair. "It *was* depressing, wasn't it, Cora?"

"It was *awful*," she said, in a small voice.

"Gideon seems to be taking it hard," Isaac mused.

Cora stirred uncomfortably in his embrace, but said nothing.

"We should pray for Hans' widow, and Gideon, and the family. They'll have a lot of tough decisions to make now."

Cora nodded, but added: "I *will*, Isaac, but I'm not going to do it now. I don't want to think about it anymore tonight, and I don't want you to think about it, either. It's a *sin* to worry, and to be sad."

Isaac smiled down at her. "That's true. I love you, Cora."

"I know that, Isaac," she teased, and twisted around to kiss him. Isaac returned her kiss with ferocious vigor, and moved down to nibble her neck, and her ear, and then swung her up in his arms and carried her off to their bedroom as she shrieked with laughter and kicked her feet.

CHAPTER TWENTY-FIVE

"It's such a tragedy," Fannie Stoltzfus said softly, and dabbed at her eyes.

Cora sat next to her in the empty school room. Class had just let out, and the children were already halfway home. The school was deserted except for the two of them. Even Mary was gone. She had said something about the post office and disappeared.

"It *was* sad," Cora agreed. "His wife looked so broken up. I felt so sorry for her."

Fannie blinked back tears, and her lips trembled. "Yes, poor Iris. We used to be close when we were children. We didn't see as much of one another after we married, but we were neighbors years ago." She shook her head.

"I don't know what I would do if Isaac –" Cora began, but couldn't bring herself to finish the words. She couldn't even *imagine* losing Isaac.

"She's in a terrible predicament," Fannie murmured. "Hans was older, and she relied on him for so much. I don't know *what* she'll do now."

She paused, and looked at Cora unhappily. "I know I shouldn't talk about it, but Iris is – Iris is *pregnant*."

"How do you know?" Cora gasped.

"My cousin saw her coming out of the doctor's in town a few months ago," Fannie replied, in a hushed voice. "The baby doctor."

"*Ohhhh*." Cora sat back in stunned amazement. "That – that's –"

Fannie shook her head. "Now she has to worry about *money*. I can't imagine anything worse.

"She must be terrified."

Cora frowned. "What do you mean, she has to worry about money? She has the business -- doesn't she?"

Fannie dabbed her eyes. "She told me herself at the funeral – and this is in confidence, Cora – that the business is in deep trouble. Gideon has been arguing with Hans about it, for *years*."

"But – that's *impossible*," Cora objected, and Fannie shook her head.

"I should be quiet, I've said too much already.

"But I can't stand the thought of Iris, having to raise her baby all alone – and having to worry about losing *everything*!"

She broke off, and fell into fresh weeping.

Cora's mouth fell open in dismay. But she was hoping for Isaac's sake that Fannie Stoltzfus was wrong.

***

When Cora got back home that evening, Isaac was there before her. But to her surprise, he was sitting outside, on the ground, with his back to the oak tree.

Cora's neck prickled with a warning of impending disaster. She walked out softly and sat down beside him on the ground.

"Are you tired of staying inside, Isaac?" she asked lightly, and took his hand. But to her dismay, he didn't answer, or look at her.

"Isaac?"

He still didn't turn his head. But presently he answered: "Gideon Miller called me into his office today, Cora. He said that the company's losing money, that it needs to be streamlined."

Cora's eyes widened. She squeezed his hand.

"He laid me off, Cora. I don't have a job anymore."

His voice had a dull, shocked tone, and Cora's heart broke for him. Her mouth crumpled. She put her hand out toward Isaac, as if she was a mother, and he a wounded child.

But Isaac *wasn't* a child, and there was nothing she could do.

"I'm glad we're paid up on the rent until August. We don't have to worry about that for a while."

Cora nodded, and stroked his hair. Isaac was trying to be brave, but she could hear the hurt and wounded pride in his voice.

Anger whisked up in her heart like fire. Isaac didn't *deserve* this. He was a true craftsman, he took pride in his work, and he worked hard. He was the last person on *earth* who should have lost his job.

"You have a *gift*, Isaac," she told him softly. "Remember that Hans Miller told you so? And everyone else knows it, too. You'll find another job. We have a little money saved. And at least we have the money from my work at the school, in the meantime."

Isaac's cheeks went a deep, dull red, and Cora was instantly sorry that she had mentioned it. She hurried to correct her mistake.

"Don't worry, Isaac," she soothed. "It will be all right. Come inside, and have your dinner."

"I'll be in, in a little while, Cora," he told her.

She could see that it would be useless to urge him. She sighed, and kissed his cheek, and climbed the stairs to the apartment door.

But she got nothing done, once she was inside. She couldn't keep herself away from the window.

***

Isaac didn't come back inside until long after dark. By that time Cora had a large, tempting dinner all laid out for him, but he picked at his food, and said little at the table.

Cora watched him helplessly. For the first time since she'd known him, there was *nothing* she could do or say to comfort him.

He went to bed without a word, and when she followed, an hour later, she found him lying on his side, facing the wall.

"I love you, Isaac," she told him softly. "And you're worrying for nothing. It will be all right."

She leaned over and kissed his bare shoulder. "I'll go to my *daed* tomorrow, Isaac, I'm sure that he –"

"I'm not going to ask your father for a job, Cora," Isaac replied quietly.

"*Your* father then, Isaac," she replied.

"I'm not going to him, either. He has no need for a woodworker."

Cora put out her hand, and caressed his back wordlessly, but he didn't respond. She knew what he was doing, she could feel it: he was drawing up a mental list of all the potential employers within 20 miles.

And he would be up before dawn the next morning to go to them.

Cora sighed and returned to her own pillow. She wouldn't trouble her husband any more: Isaac needed his rest.

But she dug her fingers into her pillow, hoping with all her heart that Gideon Miller had a *miserable, sleepless* night.

CHAPTER TWENTY-SIX

A week later, Cora rose at four o'clock and started her morning routine -- plus the new tasks she undertook to help Isaac in his job search.

She found Isaac's best suit of clothes and washed and dried and ironed and starched it, and then laid it out for him on the bed. Then she went to the kitchen and cooked a breakfast fit for a champion: pancakes and bananas and cream and fried eggs and ham and gravy.

When Isaac came to the breakfast table, he was fresh from the shower and fully dressed. He ate the breakfast she had made for him, but said little during the meal.

When he was ready to go out, Cora couldn't resist giving him a kiss. "You look *so* handsome, Isaac," she sighed, "I wish you weren't going out *at all*."

Ordinarily, a bit of flirtation would have made him smile, but this morning, Isaac wasn't in the mood for games. He just gave her a quick peck, and left.

Cora watched him go with an aching heart. Oh Lord, she prayed, please help Isaac find a job. It's not just the money.

His work means so much to him!

***

It was her day off from school, and Cora spent the late morning in their little garden. Since there was nothing more she could do for Isaac, she fended off her worry by tending the little plants that he had bought for their kitchen garden: green beans and onions, cucumbers, peppers and tomatoes. There was something about digging in the dirt with her fingers that was natural and soothing and right.

She leaned back on her heels and wiped her forehead with her arm. The sun was getting high, and a cool morning was ripening into a warm noon.

"Tending your garden?"

Cora turned her head and shaded her eyes. Katie was standing at the gate.

"Katie!" Cora stood up and ran to greet her. "I'm so glad to see you! Is Joes with you?"

"No, he's at home taking care of the baby."

"Are you sure you should be out this soon?"

Katie shook her head. "I told Joseph that I needed to get out of the house. I came into town to do a bit of shopping, and thought I'd drop in to see how you were doing, while I'm here."

Cora helped her climb the stairs. "Come inside and see the apartment. Isaac made all the furniture, by himself!"

She opened the door, and Katie nodded appreciatively. "It's beautiful, Cora," she marveled. "Joseph told me about it, but I didn't know until now just how *good* Isaac is."

Cora went pink. "I know I'm not supposed to brag," she told her, "but I can't help it. Isaac does the *best* work in town!"

In spite of her desire to stay positive, Cora couldn't keep a touch of defiance out of her voice. Katie gave her a quizzical look as she sank into a chair.

"He certainly does! Gorgeous work," she agreed.

"Even if some people don't *recognize* it," Cora replied, and then caught herself. She shook her head, and put on a smile. "Let me get you something, Katie. Maybe a cup of coffee, and some pie?"

"Thank you," Katie replied, but her eyes were on Cora's face as she bustled about the little kitchen. Katie watched her sister in law as she slapped the plates down on the table, jerked the coffee pot from its stand, and spilled some on the way to the cup.

Katie frowned faintly. "Cora – forgive me for asking, but - is everything all right?"

Cora flushed and tried to keep her face noncommittal. She nodded her head. Katie's kind expression tempted Cora to tell her everything -- but she resisted the urge. It would be disrespectful to Isaac to share her fears, and Cora was anxious to protect him.

"Everything's *fine.* Why?"

Katie was looking closely at her face. "You just seemed a bit upset, that's all. Are you sure everything is all right?"

Cora looked up and mustered her biggest, brightest smile. "Of course." She brought the coffee cup and the pie plate. "Tell me *all* the news. I've been so busy here that I haven't been home since the wedding."

Cora noticed, with relief, that Katie seemed to relax. She put the coffee cup to her lips.

"Most of the talk in town is about poor Iris Miller. She's taking Hans' death very hard."

Cora looked down at the floor and said nothing.

"I shouldn't repeat it, but there's even a rumor that she might be pregnant. I don't know whether to hope that it's true, or not. A baby would be a great comfort to Iris, of course, but also – well, a *challenge,* now that Hans is gone."

Cora scowled. "Yes, Gideon Miller inherited the family's

business, didn't he?"

"Some people are saying so, but I don't know if it's true," Katie told her.

Oh, it's true, Cora thought angrily, but restrained herself from speaking the thought out loud.

"It's sad, isn't it, Cora?" Katie wondered aloud. "How quickly things can change."

Cora gave her a quick, worried look, wondering if Katie was remembering the death of her first husband, and their son. She reached out and squeezed Katie's hand.

Katie looked up. "Oh, don't worry, Cora. I'm all right, now. But I think I know how Iris feels – a little. I may go over and visit her. I might be able to help."

Cora looked at her sister-in-law affectionately. Katie was *always* so sweet.

"Of course, you're too young to know anything about such things," Katie smiled. "You and Isaac have only been married for such a short time. But you notice it, the older you get," Katie said wistfully. "Life can be unpredictable. Sometimes it doesn't turn out the way you had hoped."

Katie shook herself, and looked up at Cora apologetically. "I'm *sorry*, Cora. Iris was on my mind, but that's no excuse to come here to rain on *your* beautiful afternoon. There is other news, if you want to hear it."

Cora nodded in relief. “Tell me!”

“Caleb is complaining that you’re not at school as much anymore. He says that he’s tired of Mary Stoltzfus and wants you to teach there *every* day.”

Cora smiled and tried to keep her tone light. “I might do that.”

Katie’s smile deepened. “And Leah Hauser *still* hasn’t accepted the fact that Isaac married *you*. She’s been moping around as if *she* was the widow in town.”

Cora tried to look attentive, but she had already tuned out.

Leah Hauser’s sulky mood was the *least* of her worries.

CHAPTER TWENTY-SEVEN

After Katie left, Cora walked down to her little backyard garden and knelt in the dirt. She returned to pulling up little weeds, but she was so troubled that she was hardly aware of what she was doing.

Katie hadn't meant to do it, but she'd *scared* her.

Because she was right. Life was unpredictable.

Last month, Hans Miller was alive and well. His wife had been happily anticipating the arrival of their baby. Isaac had been secure in his job, and had seemed to have a bright future.

This month, Hans Miller was gone. If Katie and Fannie Stoltzfus were right, his business was on the point of death, too. And Isaac was unemployed.

Life could change *overnight*.

Fear seemed to reach up out of the ground, like a hand

grabbing at Cora's throat. She thought about Iris Miller, and what Fannie Stoltzfus had said about her:

Now she has to worry about money. I can't imagine anything worse. She must be terrified.

Cora stared at the ground.

That could just as easily be *her*.

What if *she* got pregnant now? How would she and Isaac ever be able to care for a baby, without a steady paycheck?

Cora felt suddenly vulnerable. They had never even *considered* birth control, much less used it.

Her mouth turned down. The thought of using birth control made her want to burst into tears. Isaac wanted a baby -- and she *so* wanted to give him one.

But what would they do, if it happened *now*?

She knew Isaac. He wanted a baby so badly that he wouldn't care. He'd say that they needed to trust God. He'd tell her that he'd find something.

But what if that *didn't happen*?

Cora imagined it, but soon had to stop. The mental image was too painful.

If Isaac was *this* upset about not being able to provide – even temporarily – how would he feel if they had a baby, and he wasn't able to provide for it? If he had to watch others taking care of his child?

She remembered Isaac's face when he was holding little Dorathea. She imagined if it was *their* baby, and someone else had to buy her things, because they were too poor to afford them.

Cora closed her eyes.

It would *kill* Isaac. He'd just be broken.

Cora set her mouth. She couldn't let that happen. No matter what other disaster might fall, no matter how much of a risk she was taking, nothing could be worse than what she was seeing in her mind: a shamed, broken Isaac who had lost his self-respect.

Cora stood up suddenly and ran up to the apartment. She grabbed her bag off of the kitchen table and bolted back down the stairs. She didn't stop to think, or to pray, or to ask herself any further questions.

She knew what she had to do.

Her cape swirled in the air as she threw it over her head, and ran out into the little side street.

There was a back way to the place she was making for, a path that wound around the back of the buildings on the square. Cora checked before crossing the alleys, and kept herself well out of sight.

She had no intention of repeating Iris Miller's mistake.

***

Isaac came home that evening well after dark. Cora had come to recognize the expression he was wearing. He had worn it every day for over a week.

"How did it go today?" she smiled. She was trying hard to maintain a cheerful expression, but the flat, listless look in Isaac's eyes wrung her heart.

"Amos Tanner gave me an order for a wall plaque. That's all."

"But that's *something*, Isaac," she quickly replied.

"I'm not the only man that Gideon Miller laid off," Isaac sighed. "There are a lot of other shop hands searching for jobs in town."

Cora poured out a cup of coffee for him, and brought him a plate.

Isaac looked up at her gratefully. "Thank you, Cora." He put a biscuit into his mouth hungrily.

"Katie came by today," Cora said brightly. "She's starting to get out again. She said to tell you hello."

Isaac received this news in silence.

She caressed his curling hair. "You look so *tired*, baby. Why don't you change and come to bed."

"I will. You go ahead."

***

Cora undressed and went to bed. She lay in the darkness a long time, waiting for him. She followed the small sounds from the other room: Isaac pulled off his shoes. He went to the kitchen and got something out of the refrigerator. The kitchen bench creaked as he sat down.

He didn't move for more than 20 minutes.

Cora lay very quiet. A small sound wafted in from the kitchen, a low murmur almost too faint to hear.

Cora pulled her mouth down.

Isaac was praying.

She rolled over and buried her face in the pillow.

CHAPTER TWENTY-EIGHT

Cora climbed the steps to the little landing wearily.

It had been the last day of school before the summer break, and there had been a lot to do. The children had been excited and very active.

Plus, Mary had taken a rare day off. Fannie Stoltzfus had smiled mysteriously, and hinted that it might have something to do with Seth Troyer, but Cora had been too preoccupied with her own troubles to wonder much about her friend.

It had been a tiring day, and she was glad to be home. Cora stopped at the top of the stairs to catch her breath.

She opened the door -- and was shocked to see that Isaac was already there. He was sitting in a chair facing the door. Almost as if he was *waiting* for her.

He lifted his face, and Cora froze. She noticed several things, all at once:

He was *crushed*. This was – this was something far beyond even their money worries, she could see that instantly.

He was *furious*. His eyes had practically changed color. They were a strange, dark, gunmetal gray.

He was furious *at her*.

"Isaac?" she stammered, and took a tentative step toward him.

He stared at her with such a hard look on his face that Cora felt her lower lip start to tremble.

He was holding something in his hand, and Cora looked down at it.

It was the birth control she had gotten from town. It was lying in his palm like a crushed packet of crackers.

How had he found it?

She lifted pleading eyes to his face, but he looked down at the floor and said nothing, as if he couldn't trust himself to speak to her.

Cora dropped her bag and flung herself onto her knees in front of him.

"Isaac, don't be *angry*. Darling, let me explain –"

But for the first time in his life, Isaac rejected her embrace. He blocked her hands, and she fell aside onto the floor.

"How could you do this to me?" he said quietly.

Cora lifted sorrowful eyes to his face. "Isaac, I haven't *taken* any of them!"

"You were going to go on birth control without even *telling* me."

Cora bit her lip. "I'm sorry, Isaac, *please* don't hate me, I was just – I was scared."

His lips tightened to a thin, straight line. He nodded grimly. "You've hidden things from me before, Cora, but the cell phone was *nothing* compared to this."

"I was trying to keep us from getting into *trouble*, Isaac," she replied, in a small, tearful voice.

"Have I ever done this to you, Cora? Haven't I always asked you what you wanted, what was important to you?"

Cora bowed her head. She nodded miserably.

"I can't believe you did this to me," he replied evenly. "I've been patient with you, Cora. I've made allowances for you. *Excuses,* even. But this – *this* is –" He suddenly threw the little packet against the wall with all his strength.

Cora collapsed on the floor, weeping.

"How can I trust you, Cora?" he wondered aloud. "You make promises, but you don't keep them. You tell me you love me -- but you don't tell me the truth."

"I *do* love you!" Cora sobbed.

"You're spoiled, Cora Lapp," he told her, and now his voice held grief. "But I had hoped that for something as important as *this*, you'd love me enough to think of what I wanted, too."

"Oh, Isaac, I *was* thinking of you!" she sobbed. "If we had a baby and we couldn't *support* it, you'd be –"

She stopped herself, and put a hand to her mouth. She rolled horrified eyes to her husband's face.

Isaac's face had been grim and pale, but now it was a dull red.

"I see."

"Oh, no, Isaac, I meant –"

He nodded. "I know what you meant, Cora."

"Isaac, I swear, I didn't mean that like it sounded. Darling, don't be angry, I –"

He stood up.

"You don't have to worry, Cora."

Cora's eyes widened in sudden fear. She scrambled up off the floor and reached for his arm.

"Isaac –"

"We're not going to be having children any time soon. I'm

leaving."

"Isaac, please!" she sobbed.

He reached for his hat. "And you don't have to worry about the money so much, Cora. I found a job today. I'll be working for Levi Hauser this week. Out at his farm."

Cora stared at him in dismay. "You're going to work for *Leah Hauser's* father!"

"That's right, Cora. It was all I could find."

"Oh – oh no, Isaac!" she cried. "I can't stand to think of – of Leah Hauser *staring* at you while you work! She's *always* been –"

"I'll be staying there while the job lasts."

Cora set her mouth. "I *know* that I made a mistake, Isaac. You have a right to be angry, I admit it! But it's wrong to tease me with Leah Hauser. You can't go out there, I'll go crazy!"

"Goodbye, Cora."

"Isaac!"

He walked out the door and down the stairs. Cora watched him go in disbelief. She could barely keep herself from running down the stairs after him.

When the sound of his footsteps had faded, Cora slid down onto the floor and collapsed in a heap, sobbing.

When she raised her eyes, they fell on the shattered disc of pink plastic lying just under the window.

CHAPTER TWENTY-NINE

Cora spent a miserable night. She didn't even go to bed, because it would have been useless to even try to sleep.

The next morning she was grateful that the school year was over for the summer, because she couldn't have faced a roomful of children with her swollen eyes and red nose.

But the prospect of spending the day alone in that desolate apartment was more than she could bear. If she'd thought there was any hope that Isaac would come back, she would've stayed: but there was no hope.

She acknowledged, to her shame, that Isaac always did just what he said he'd do.

She went to the bathroom, and took a shower, and tried to wash a night of crying off of her face. She dried her hair, pinned it up, and dressed.

She was going over to Joes and Katie's house. She

suddenly longed for Joe's good sense, and for Katie's soothing voice.

***

She was just pinning her cap over the hair, when the sound of frantic knocking outside made her drop everything and run to the door.

But when she threw it open, to her disappointment, it *wasn't* Isaac.

It was Fannie Stoltzfus.

"Why, Fannie!" Cora stammered. To her surprise, Fannie's eyes were as swollen, and her nose as red, as her own.

"Come in -- is something the matter?" Cora blurted. She had never seen her placid schoolteacher so distraught.

"Let me get you a cup of tea," Cora offered, but Fannie waved it away.

"Mary's gone!" she told Cora, in a quavering voice.

Cora stared at her. "*What*?"

"Mary's gone! She left me a note telling me that she's flying off to *Paris*, of all places! Did you know anything about this, Cora Muller?" the older woman demanded.

"*No,* I promise, Fannie! Mary never said anything about going there to me!"

Fannie removed her glasses and wiped them on her apron. "She wasn't in her room this morning. When I went up, her bed hadn't been slept in. But she left a note."

She handed Cora a letter. Cora took it in her hands and read:

Dear Mamm and Daed:

I'm sorry to tell you like this, but it was the best way I could think of to do it. I got a letter a few days ago. I won first prize in that essay contest I entered. They're giving me a week in Paris.

Cora couldn't repress an excited exclamation: "Oh, Fannie, *she won a trip to Paris!"*

Fannie broke out into muffled sobbing, and Cora added, in a chastened tone: "*Oh*. Oh – I'm sorry, Fannie."

I know that I might get in trouble, and I'm sorry about that for your sake. But this is my dream, and I'm going to go for it. I couldn't lie to you, and tell you that I was going somewhere else, when I wasn't.

Cora went red, and swallowed the guilty lump that rose in her throat.

But if I get in trouble, I'll just say that this was my choice, and that you didn't know anything about it, because you didn't.

Cora felt tears pricking her lids. That explained why Mary

had never said a word about it to *her*.

I'm sorry if I've upset you, but please try to understand, and be happy for me. I've dreamed about this trip for my whole life, and now it's coming true.

Cora looked up at her guest.

"Mary never breathed a *word* of this to me, Fannie," she told her. "I guess she didn't want to get me in trouble."

"I blame myself," Fannie told her. "I *knew* she had entered the contest, and I encouraged her. I thought it would help her be a little more outgoing. But I never thought that she'd *win* -- and run away!"

"Well, but Fannie, maybe it won't turn out so badly," Cora soothed. "Mary *said* that she'd always wanted to do this. It *is* her rumspringa, after all. Maybe she just needs to get it out of her system."

"She's going to a foreign country, *all alone*," Fannie sobbed. "I can't even let myself *imagine* all the terrible things that might happen."

Cora raised her brows. She couldn't help remembering her day trip to New York with Mary, and how her scrawny friend had shoved a mugger out into oncoming traffic.

"It's only a few days. I think she'll be all right. And the people running the contest will probably send someone to the airport to meet her, won't they?"

"Oh, I don't know. I can only hope so," Fannie replied. "I'm sorry, Cora, I didn't mean to burst in on you like this. It's just that I thought you might be able to tell me something."

"I am," Cora told her. "I can tell you that Mary's a smart girl, Fannie. And she's brave. I think she's going to be just fine."

Fannie nodded. "You're a comfort to me, Cora," Fannie told her, patting her arm. "I pray you're right."

"Don't let your imagination run away with you, Fanny," Cora said kindly. "Mary will be back in a week or so, and everything will be all right."

Fannie Stoltzfus gave her a grateful hug, and went her way: but after Cora had closed the door behind her, she frowned.

Don't let your imagination run away with you.

She couldn't help thinking of Isaac, out at Levi Hauser's farm, for a *whole week*. She saw him working out in the barn, his muscles rippling under his shirt as he sawed, and drove nails, and carried lumber.

She saw a tight, angry expression on his face when he thought of her, and imagined him muttering under his breath.

And then she saw a smiling Leah Hauser, skipping out to the barn to give him lemonade and cake.

And anything *else* she possibly could.

Cora couldn't even bear to let herself dwell on where Isaac might be sleeping. In a room with a lock, she *hoped.*

Don't let your imagination run away with you.

Cora's mouth turned down. It was easy advice to give -- and very hard advice to take.

CHAPTER THIRTY

"Voici votre chambre, mademoiselle."

The bellboy opened the door to Mary's hotel suite in Paris. He set her luggage down on the carpeted floor.

Mary stepped across the threshold and gazed around with wide, round eyes. It was *breathtaking. Palatial.*

A wrought-iron chandelier glittered overhead. Ceiling-high windows were covered in silken brocade. There was a huge sitting room, complete with a couch and Louis XVI chairs and a desk and an entertainment center. And even *that* wasn't all: there were other doors on the far side of the suite. The bellboy crossed the room and opened the door to what looked like a vast bedroom, and another to a bathroom so huge that it looked like it might contain a *pool.*

Then he turned, stepped to the windows, and pulled the drapes back with a *snap*. He threw open the wrought-iron doors to the balcony. They swung apart to reveal a breathtaking vista of graceful trees and Parisian rooftops.

Mary's mouth fell open.

The Eiffel Tower *itself* gleamed faintly in the far distance.

The bellboy returned to her, and Mary recovered herself enough to dig in her bag and to press a tip into his gloved hand.

"Merci, mademoiselle."

He saluted her, and the door swung shut behind him.

She had arrived *at last*.

***

Mary kicked off her cruel, beautiful heels and let her toes sink into the plush carpet. The airplane trip had been long and exhausting, but now that she was in Paris at last, Mary was so excited that she felt as if she could stay up all night.

She circled around, looking up at the carved ceiling, and the delicate wallpaper, and the – yes, they were real oil paintings! – on the wall.

She drifted over to the elegant desk, and to her surprise, there was an envelope there addressed to her. She tore it open and pulled out a heavy sheet of paper.

Mademoiselle Stoltzfus,

Congratulations once again, and welcome to Paris!

We hope that you will enjoy your stay in our city. You are of course free to explore in any manner you choose, but we have taken the liberty of engaging a tour professional to be your personal guide to Paris. Mignon will be available to help you as early as tomorrow morning at 8 a.m., if you choose.

Mignon is a lifelong Parisienne and will be happy to answer questions. You may reach her at the enclosed number.

Congratulations once again. We hope that this will be only the first of many visits to our beautiful city.

***

A discreet tap from outside interrupted her amazement. Mary went to the door.

A waiter stood there with a fully laden dinner cart. Mary's mouth fell open.

"Avec les compliments de la maison, mademoiselle."

She stepped aside, and he rolled the cart just in front of the dining table. He handed her a printed menu with a gesture of extreme politeness.

"Oh…well…um. I *see*…uh…duck *foie gras* canapés. And beluga caviar…and nicoise salad…and fillet of beef. And a cheese assortment, a bottle of champagne, and crème brulee! Thank you so much!"

The waiter was as impassive as a statue as he lifted the

bottle and uncorked it. Mary watched in fascination as he served portions of each little dainty, arranging them painstakingly on china plates and setting them out just *so*.

"Bon appétit, mademoiselle."

Mary was so overwhelmed that she forgot even to tip him. As soon as the door had closed behind him, she sat down at the table and shook out the napkin. It felt strange and wonderful to eat a meal that neither she, nor anyone else she knew, had made.

Mary poured out a glass of the pale, sparkling wine and lifted it to her lips. Tiny little bubbles tickled her nose and her throat as she swallowed.

It tasted wonderful.

She took a bigger swallow and pulled the plate toward her. The beef was like nothing she had ever tasted; it melted in her mouth like butter. The salad was crisp and cold and fresh and the duck *foie gras* was rich and delicious on a cracker.

Mary poured herself another glass of champagne.

The cheese assortment was even better than the cheeses her family made at home, and to Mary's mind, there was no higher praise. They were smooth and rich and creamy and delicate and delicious.

***

Suddenly it was too much to enjoy all by herself.

Mary took her wine glass and padded over to the little desk.

She picked up the hotel telephone and dialed Cora's cell phone number.

But to Mary's disappointment, a smooth female voice came over the line and announced: "We're sorry, that number is no longer in service."

Mary twisted her mouth to one side. Cora's husband must have found her phone.

She took another swallow of champagne. There was only one other person at home who had a phone number for her to call.

She put a hand to her mouth and giggled. *That silly little worm, Seth Troyer.*

***

The phone rang for a long time, but just when Mary thought she might have to hang up, the line clicked to life.

"Hello?"

"Guess who *this* is!"

There was a stunned silence. "*Mary*?"

"Guess where I am?"

"Oh, Mary, I'm so glad to hear from you!" Seth yelped. "Your parents are *beside* themselves!"

"Seth, do me a favor, please tell them I'm okay," Mary murmured.

"I will," he promised. "I still can't believe you flew to Paris on your own!"

Mary took another sip of wine. She felt as if a million little tiny bubbles were rising from her chin to the top of her brain.

"What is it *like* over there, Mary?" Seth asked.

"*Beautiful*, Seth. My room is as big as the first floor of our house. And I can see the Eiffel Tower from the window!"

"I wish I could be there to see it with you, Mary," Seth said shyly.

"It's strange, Seth, very strange. It's too much, just *too much*, but also kind of pretty. And everyone dresses *very* English. They all have *beautiful* shoes."

There was another long silence on the other end.

"Mary, are you okay? You sound a little…"

Mary shook her head back and forth. "Of *course* I'm okay. *Silly*." She started to chuckle, and the phone fell out of her hand.

CHAPTER THIRTY-ONE

Mary woke up at five a.m. the next morning, as usual. But the silken hotel coverlet swirled around her like a cloud, and instead of getting up, she just groaned and burrowed back into its downy embrace.

An hour later, she woke up again. It was now at least six thirty, because her bedroom windows showed the sun just rising over the rooftops of Paris.

Mary blinked and gradually remembered where she was.

Then she smiled a wide, slow smile, and threw the covers back.

***

Mignon Avril was sitting in the hotel lobby at 8 a.m. sharp, just as promised. She was a tiny, elfin woman of about thirty. Her hair was as black as ink and cut in a chic but *very* short bob. Large hoop earrings dangled from her ears, and she wore an elegant silk scarf, casually tossed over a fitted long sleeved shirt and tailored designer slacks.

Mary's first opinion of Mignon was that she was the most elegantly dressed woman she had ever seen in her life.

"Bonjour, Marie."

"*Bonjour*," Mary replied shyly. She tucked a wisp of hair behind her ear self-consciously.

"Congratulations on winning the essay contest," Mignon smiled. "It wasn't an easy thing to do, I'm sure! And I know you must be eager to get out and see the city. What sights would you especially like to see?"

Mary felt a little dazed. She still couldn't believe this was really happening.

"The Louvre, of course, and the Eiffel Tower, and the *Arc de Triomphe*. And Versailles, and Notre Dame, and –"

"Stop, *stop*," Mignon threw up her hands, "one at a time! Let's take the Louvre first. You could spend the whole day, just on that. We'll take the museum first. I'm glad you're an early riser – the lines aren't as long in the morning.

"Have you had your breakfast yet?"

Mary shook her head.

"Neither have I. We can stop by a bakery I know. They make the best croissants in the city."

***

For Mary Stoltzfus, the next hour was like a dream, a lovely dream of a warm, tiny shop fragrant of bread, tiny cups filled with delicious coffee, and jewel-like pastries that melted in her mouth.

Then the frantic taxi ride to the museum, and Mignon's clever short cut side entrance that whisked them past all the lines.

And then it really *was* a dream: Mary's eyes opened wide to allow it all to come streaming in: the soft, beautiful pastoral landscapes, the 16th century still lifes that looked real enough to touch, the classical paintings with simpering cherubs and half-dressed shepherds and frolicking animals.

And the clothing: the *beautiful* clothing. Mary found herself staring at the minute details: a fine lace cuff that was almost transparently sheer. A row of shimmering pearls against a silken gown. A ruby ring, glowing on a pale, delicate hand.

It was so *womanly*.

When they finally left, late in the afternoon, Mary felt dazed. She was silent during the taxi ride back to the hotel. The cumulative effect of the Louvre was like a shining wave, cresting and breaking over her head. She felt as if she had fallen under water.

***

The next morning, Mignon was waiting for her in her lobby, right on time.

"Where would you like to go today?" Mignon was asking her.

Mary rolled her eyes to her fashionable host. "I know I told you a lot of places, but I want to see them *later*. Today I want to go to a *salon*. I want to get my hair cut, *just like yours*. And then I want to go shopping for *makeup* and *clothes*."

Mignon's lips curved slightly upward. "*Alors*! I can arrange that. Paris is the best of *all* cities for fashion."

She half-turned in the seat and gave Mary an appraising glance.

"*And* beauty."

***

An hour later Mary found herself sitting in a salon chair as a woman with orange hair and a parrot tattoo cupped her face in her hands.

"I think it could work," she mused. "The style would look good with her face shape. Of course it will be a *drastic* change."

She pulled her hands away, and Mary's dark, flowing hair tumbled all the way down onto the floor.

The hairdresser met Mary's eyes in the mirror.

"Are you *sure*?"

Mary set her lips and nodded.

The woman laughed, and snapped the shears a few times in the air before cutting Mary's hair just under the ears.

It seemed to Mary as if the stylist was never going to finish. She kept her eyes closed as the woman snipped here, and combed there, and measured, and snipped again. She was afraid to watch, afraid that her impulsive decision would turn out to be a terrible mistake. What if it looked terrible, or worse -- *funny*?

But when the hairdresser had finished at last, and swung the chair around to let Mary and Mignon see the full effect, Mary gasped. Her hair was now extremely wispy and short -- what the hairdresser called *gamine.*

Mary stared at the mirror with round, dark eyes. A complete stranger was staring back at her.

But Mignon Avril nodded approvingly.

"Tres chic!"

Mary turned her head this way and that, appraising the result.

She looked – she looked –

The hairdresser fluffed Mary's hair in triumph.

"*Magnifique*!" she announced.

CHAPTER THIRTY-TWO

Isaac Muller bent over a work bench in Levi Hauser's shop, rhythmically planing wood. It was good that he could practically do this task in his sleep, because ever since he'd come to Levi Hauser's, he *had* been sleepwalking. His mind was not on his job.

He pushed the sander out over the boards. No matter where he looked, he saw Cora's beautiful face, crumpled up in grief. His dreams had been haunted by her voice, calling out to him.

He pushed the sander again. Maybe he *had* been too harsh. He had been very angry with her, not willing to listen. She'd done something wrong, but only because she had been frightened.

He had been frightened, too.

When he last saw her, she'd been sobbing, distraught. He had shown her no pity, and had left without a backward glance.

He stopped work and looked down at his hands.

Last night in his dreams, Cora's slender arms had reached for him, and her eyes had sparkled like stars. She had covered his face with kisses and disintegrated into laughter when he took her in his arms.

He felt guilty suddenly, like a bad husband. No one was kinder or more well-meaning than Cora. When she got into trouble, it was mostly because she was trying to help someone else.

He heard her voice again: "Isaac, I was thinking of you! If we had a baby and we couldn't support it, you'd be –"

He started planing again.

It was hard for him to admit to himself. But maybe he'd been angry because Cora's fears had made him feel like a *bad provider*.

Maybe he'd been angry because she'd accidentally hurt his *pride* – that thing he wasn't supposed to indulge.

Maybe Cora was right. If she became pregnant now, his joy would shine as bright as the sun.

But as time went on, and if there was still no money to support the baby, that joy would soon be dimmed with grief.

And terrible *shame*.

As bad as it had sounded for her to keep this from him,

maybe she *had* been trying to spare him.

He shook his head and frowned.

But *even so* -- he was still reeling from the shock of finding that tiny box. It had felt like a punch in the stomach.

How could Cora's upturned face shine like an angel's – how could her eyes seem to glow with innocent love – when *all the time*, she was deceiving him? When she *knew – she had known all along –*

He stopped working and closed his eyes.

***

At lunchtime, Isaac stopped work to wash up. There was a tiny room at the back of the shop, just large enough to hold a bed and a bathroom. It was his temporary home for the week.

When he came out again, his eyebrows twitched up in surprise.

Leah Hauser was standing at the workbench with a hot lunch all laid out.

"You must be starving, Isaac," Leah smiled, shaking out a napkin. "Mamm sent me out here to bring you some lunch."

"Oh – thank you, Leah."

"It's not much, I'm afraid – just some of that spicy sausage we made, and some gravy dumplings, and a little creamed spinach, and cornbread. Oh, and a pot of coffee. You must be thirsty."

The scent of fried sausage wafted to Isaac's nose. "It smells wonderful. Tell your Mamm thank you."

"I added a piece of my shoofly pie, too," Leah smiled, sliding another plate toward him. "I remember how you always used to *love* it."

Isaac shot her a look as he pulled up a chair.

"Are you going to join me, Leah?" he asked politely.

"Oh no, you go ahead, I've already had my lunch. But I hope you don't mind if I stay for a few minutes. I haven't seen you in ages. *We're* still friends, I hope."

Isaac shot her a quick look, and said nothing.

"I heard about the cutbacks at the shop. It was *so* unfair to you."

She lowered her eyes. "But it might be a blessing in disguise, Isaac. You know, you *could* work here for longer than a week, if you wanted. Daed is planning to add tool sheds and swings and other things to his garden supply line. If he's happy with your work, he might hire you *permanently*."

Isaac's face remained impassive, and she pressed:

"You're the *best* woodwright in the state, and everyone knows it. Gideon Miller is a *fool*."

Isaac shook his head. "He did what he had to do, Leah. It's what everyone does."

Leah's dark eyes found his face.

"Yes, I *know*."

She sidled closer, and her voice dropped. "Ever since you got married, I've done what I *had* to do, Isaac. I've lain awake in the dark, thinking about you *every* night."

"Leah –"

"I can't help it." She reached out and put her hand on his. "I love you, Isaac, I *always* have. I can't pretend that I don't. Don't you ever think of me, sometimes? Don't you feel *anything* for me, Isaac?"

Isaac pulled his hand away and looked down. "Leah, maybe you should go back inside," he murmured. "If your father were to come out and see my hand in yours, he'd be very angry, and I wouldn't blame him."

"Are *you* angry, Isaac?" Leah pressed.

Isaac didn't meet her eyes. "I'm a married man, Leah."

Leah smiled faintly and withdrew, but not before whispering:

"*Hmm*. I thought you were going to tell me that you were a *happily* married man, Isaac."

CHAPTER THIRTY-THREE

"Cora," Isaac murmured.

Moonlight slanted in through the window of the little bedroom and painted his pillow with light.

His head tossed. "*Sweet angel.*"

Cora was lying on the floor of their apartment, weeping. Her bright hair flowed over her shoulders like the wings of some golden bird. Her beautiful arms lay limp on the floor like broken reeds.

He was trying to lift her to her feet. "Cora, don't cry," he was saying. "I'm sorry I was harsh with you. Look at me."

She raised her bright blue eyes to his face, and they burned like two stars. "Oh, Isaac, you know I'd *never* hurt you," she was saying.

He pulled her gently into his arms and put a finger under her chin. She lifted her face to him like a flower and pressed her lips against his. They were as soft and fragrant and yielding as rose petals.

"*Cora*," he murmured, savoring the silkiness of her mouth, the sweet pressure of her slender body against his. Her heart fluttered against his chest like a dove beating its wings against the bars of a cage.

That sweet fluttering beat on his chest until his own heart thrummed in unison. The sound of it filled his brain. Even his ears.

Isaac tossed his head.

His eyes slowly opened. It took him a long moment to remember that he was in Levi Hauser's work shed, and not his own home.

He put a hand to his head, frowned, and closed his eyes.

"Isaac!"

He opened his eyes again. He hadn't dreamed it: someone was outside, knocking furtively at the door.

He threw the covers back and rubbed his face groggily.

"Who is it?"

"Open the door, it's an emergency!"

Isaac reached over his head and pulled down a bathrobe. He shrugged into it and pulled the belt tight.

"Who is it?" he grumbled.

"Isaac, it's Leah! You have to come help -- there's a *fire*!"

Isaac's brows rushed together. He opened the door quickly.

He looked around anxiously, but the shop was as safe and serene as it had been when he had left it.

But there was definitely one thing on fire: *Leah Hauser*.

She was standing in the doorway of his little room, dressed in the sheerest of cotton shifts. The moonlight behind her on the shop floor shone through it, and it was crystal clear that she had nothing on underneath.

As soon as the door was open, she threw herself into his arms.

"Leah, *what are you doing*? Let go of me!"

Leah clung to him and pressed her lips to his in a passionate kiss. "Kiss me, Isaac," she breathed, and grabbed his neck. "Give me just one night to remember. I'll live on it the rest of my life!"

He took her hands and unhooked them from his neck. "Leah, *go back to bed*," he hissed urgently, "and *act like you should*. I'm not in love with you, and we'll both be ruined if anyone sees you here!" He looked over her shoulder anxiously.

Tears fell onto his hands. "I don't ask that you love me,

Isaac," Leah whimpered. "But for God's sake, be kind to me *just once*. Cora Lapp will have you all the rest of her life. Let me be with you, just *one* night!"

She pressed herself against him again.

To Isaac's horror, her naked body, pressed so close, began to stir him. He grappled with her hands.

"Leah, *go away*. You know better than to ask me this."

Leah laughed into his neck. "You *do* want me, Isaac," she gasped, "and I want *you*. Let me in, we can lock the door, no one will know! And I promise I'll *never* tell."

Her lips on his burned like fire, and her body was warm and yielding. Isaac hesitated -- then wavered.

He put a hand to her hair, feeling its silky softness. She wrapped herself around him, and a wave of weakness flowed through him.

"*Kiss me*, Isaac!"

CHAPTER THIRTY-FOUR

Fannie Stoltzfus sat in the middle of her living room. Her face was drawn and ashen. Her hands were clasped together in her lap so tightly that her knuckles looked white.

Three parent representatives of the school board sat facing her: Berta Eckhard, Elizabeth Hauser, and Martha Hottstetler – *the bishop's wife*.

"We called this meeting because some of the parents have expressed concern," Martha Hottstetler said gently. "Mary has been a fine teacher, no one disputes it. But something seems to have happened to change her. She used to be a shy, quiet girl, very good and obedient.

"But in the last few months, she has begun to dress and behave differently."

Fannie looked down at the floor. "Yes, she has dressed differently, but many children do, on their *rumspringa*."

“Mary holds a position of trust. Teachers have to do more than simply pass on information,” Martha Hottstetler replied. “They have to model Amish values. We can’t have someone teaching the children who comes back from Paris with her hair cut as short as a boy’s, and wearing makeup and English clothes.”

Fannie bit her lip, and was silent.

“It’s not *Mary’s* fault,” Elizabeth Hauser sniffed. “Mary was as good as gold until she took up with that *Cora Lapp*. When you said that you’d offered Cora a job at the school, Fannie, I told you then that you’d live to rue the day. And now it looks like the chickens have come home to roost. That girl is only good for causing trouble!”

“Cora has been a wonderful teacher, Elizabeth,” Fannie objected. “The children love her, and she helped avert a tragedy that day we had the fire.”

Martha Hottstetler felt moved to intervene. “I don’t know of anything against Cora,” she said quietly. “She seems to have settled down quite a bit since her marriage. She obeys the *Ordnung*, she lives quietly.”

Her eyes returned to Fannie. “But Mary needs to understand that she has to respect our values, if she wants to continue teaching. Why don’t you call them in?”

Fannie nodded and rose. When she returned, Mary and Cora trailed behind her.

The other women stared openmouthed.

Mary's hair was bobbed, moussed and dyed black. Her eyes were rimmed in eyeliner, her brows had been plucked and shaped, and she was wearing red lipstick. Her clothes clung to her slender body, and her jeans hugged her hips about two inches below her waist.

Cora, by contrast, was a model Amish woman. Her blonde head was covered by a snowy white cap, her blue dress and apron were the same cut as every other woman's in town.

Martha Hottstetler motioned toward the sofa. "Sit down, girls." She turned her eyes to Mary. "Mary Stoltzfus, you were raised in this community. I don't think I need to explain why we're here. You know as well as anyone that you can't teach at school looking the way you do."

Mary looked down at her shoes.

"If you repent of this rebelliousness, and let your hair grow back out, then you may return to teaching. But if you do not, you may no longer be a teacher at our school. Do you understand?"

Mary nodded.

Martha sighed. "You're a good teacher, Mary," she added kindly. "I would hate to see you step down. But we have no choice."

Up to this point, Cora had listened in silence. But now she

was frowning.

"It wasn't *Mary's* fault," she objected.

Elizabeth Hauser pursed her lips, nodded, and threw Fannie a significant glance.

"It was *my* fault, not Mary's. I – I gave her catalogs full of English clothes, and encouraged her to order them."

Mary turned her head. "*Cora* –"

"I gave her my cell phone number, and invited her to get a cell phone herself."

Fannie Stoltzfus stared at her, aghast.

"*I* was the one who messed her up. It's *my* fault – not Mary's."

Mary interjected: "That's not true. She didn't force me to do it, it was *my* decision. I didn't tell Cora anything about going to Paris, she had no part in that –"

"You understand that this means you're liable for church discipline, Cora Muller?" Martha Hottstetler said quietly.

Cora looked down and nodded.

"There will have to be a meeting to determine what the next steps should be. But the *both* of you may consider yourselves barred from teaching, out of communion, and in need of repentance."

She rose.

"Fannie, we'll be back in touch with you later."

The women rose. Fannie stood up and followed them to the door.

After they had disappeared, she turned around to face Cora.

"Cora Muller, I –" She looked down at her feet. "Please just *go*."

Cora exchanged a tearful glance with Mary, put a hand to her mouth, and fled the house.

End of Lancaster County Second Chances – Book 4

Thank you for Reading!

LANCASTER COUNTY SECOND CHANCES 5

CHAPTER ONE

Isaac Muller staggered back against the workshop door. Leah Hauser pressed her barely clothed body right into his and brushed her lips across his neck. The touch of Leah's tongue on his skin sent crazy electricity branching deep through his body.

Isaac's mind blanked out. That instant, Leah's supple body and exploratory kisses were the only things in it. She was begging him for pleasure, murmuring obscenities, raking his back like a clawing cat.

Isaac closed his eyes and let that split-second of insanity reel out. Leah's hands moved down his chest, fretting the flimsy belt that kept his robe around his body. Another instant, and his robe would be on the floor, they would both be naked, and it would be too late to turn back.

But though his mind was stunned, Isaac's heart revived. The thought of Cora flared in the darkness and flowered into a thousand bright memories.

He imagined Cora's beautiful blue eyes—but now the sweet, trusting look that he loved was gone. In its place was the dull, dead look of disillusionment and betrayal.

He had only an instant to decide.

Isaac pulled his mouth away.

***

He clamped his hands around Leah's shoulders and thrust her firmly out from him. "Go *back to the house*, Leah," he said sternly. "I told you that I'm a married man. A *happily married man*."

Even though Isaac had only used a fraction of his strength, Leah stumbled violently backwards and only saved herself from falling by grabbing at the work table.

"Go away and stop following me," he panted. "*Find a man of your own*."

Leah leaned heavily against the work table. Gradually she gathered her robe, and her composure.

"Your mouth says one thing, Isaac Muller," she replied breathlessly. "But your *body* says another. I know you can't admit it, even to yourself, but *you want me.*

"That bride of yours will drag you down. What kind of life can you make for yourself here, with *Cora Lapp*? She's a train wreck, Isaac. She'll ruin whatever you try to build.

"Sooner or later you'll see that you married the wrong woman. It might not be tonight. *But you'll come to me, Isaac.*

"And I'll be waiting."

Isaac made a tired, waving motion with one hand. "Go back to the house, Leah," he murmured, and turned into the little bedroom. He closed the door behind him and turned the lock.

He could hear Leah crying softly on the other side of the door for a few minutes, and then the sound of the outer door closing announced that she had given up at last.

But Isaac sat in the dark, wide-eyed and panting, for a long time.

Then he gathered his wits, dressed, and packed.

***

It was deep night when Isaac emerged from the little shop bedroom. He walked across the yard, to Levi Hauser's front porch, and slipped a small handwritten note under the door.

Words of apology, of a family crisis, of the need to break off their contract. He would think of the details later.

The important thing was to put as much distance between

himself and Leah as he could.

The moon was high and bright in the sky, and a chill mist was rising from the meadows. It was almost ten miles back to town, and it was going to be a long, cold walk.

But staying in that cramped, tiny shop was impossible now.

Isaac shook his head. One minute, he was sleeping peacefully in his bed – the next, Leah Hauser was plastered over his chest and doing her best to untie his robe.

He wondered if it was real, or if he was still dreaming. But the rocky road underneath his feet and the cold night air were real enough.

It had all happened so *fast.*

Isaac pulled his mouth into a tight line. Leah had ambushed him when he was half-asleep. She had been calculating, dishonest. For an instant he was angry, but the feeling quickly faded.

It was useless to be angry at Leah.

He was the one who had really failed. He should've told Leah long ago that he had no feelings for her. She had clearly been confused by his silence.

It was painful to admit, but looking back, he *had* been flattered to have two beautiful women like Cora and Leah fighting for his attention. Whenever he had been worried about losing Cora, all he had to do was remember how she looked when Leah Hauser even *talked* to him, and he had been comforted.

When they'd quarreled during their courtship, he had once tried to make Cora jealous by encouraging Leah. And it had worked too well. Cora had overreacted in fear and anger and now Leah was bitter and full of revenge.

He had been wrong to do it, and now he was paying a price.

It was *his* fault, really.

A full-body wave of shame surged up from Isaac's feet to his hair. He wondered why he'd hesitated -- why he'd allowed Leah to crawl over him.

Now, under the cool, sane night sky, he was shaken to think that he'd been *seconds* from destroying everything he loved.

It was going to be hard to meet Cora's eyes, once he got home. He had let Leah pin him against the door, and kiss him, and if he hadn't come to his senses quickly, he would this minute be lying in the dark, wrestling with bitter regret.

He set his jaw. He'd have to tell Cora, tell her *everything*, to preserve his own self-respect, and her trust. But nothing would hurt her more than knowing that he had allowed Leah Hauser to...

He imagined the look in her eyes, and quick tears sprang to his own. Cora was the last person on earth he would ever want to hurt -- but that was *exactly* what was about to happen.

She had tried to warn him, even begged him not to go to the Hauser's. But he hadn't been willing to listen. Now he wished that he *had*.

An owl called in the meadow off to the right of the road. Farther off, its mate replied.

Isaac transferred his tool bag from one arm to the other, and trudged doggedly along the road, praying that when he got back home, Cora would still be there... and that she would still be with him, after she found out what had just happened...

Thank you for Reading!

I hope you enjoyed reading this sample as much as I loved writing it! If so, look for Lancaster County Second Chances 5 in eBook and Paperback format.

All the best,

Ruth

ABOUT THE AUTHOR

Ruth Price is a Pennsylvania native and devoted mother of four. After her youngest set off for college, she decided it was time to pursue her childhood dream to become a fiction writer. Drawing inspiration from her faith, her husband and love of her life Harold, and deep interest in Amish culture that stemmed from a childhood summer spent with her family on a Lancaster farm, Ruth began to pen the stories that had always jabbered away in her mind. Ruth believes that art at its best channels a higher good, and while she doesn't always reach that ideal, she hopes that her readers are entertained and inspired by her stories.

FIC 09/13/2016 3CLY00027746
PRI
Price, Ruth
Second Chances #4

CPSIA information can be obtained
at www.ICGtesting.com
Printed in the USA
LVOW04s0715110916
504099LV00011B/101/P

9 781515 375869